D1118777

THE DEEP BLUE MEMORY

THE BASQUE SERIES

The Deep Blue Memory

Monique Urza

 University of Nevada Press

Reno / Las Vegas / London

Basque Series Editor: William A. Douglass

A list of books in the series appears at the end of the text.

The paper used in this book meets the requirements of American National Standard for Information Sciences—Permanence of Paper for Printed Library Materials, ANSI Z39.48.1984. Binding materials were selected for strength and durability.

Library of Congress Cataloging-in-Publication Data

Urza, Monique, 1953–

The deep blue memory / Monique Urza.

p. cm. — (Basque series)

ISBN 0-87417-212-8

1. Basque Americans—History—Fiction. I. Title. II. Series.

PS3571.R95D43 1993

813'.54—dc20 92-29029 CIP

University of Nevada Press, Reno, Nevada 89557 USA

Book design by Mary Mendell

Printed in the United States of America

9 8 7 6 5 4 3 2 1

For my father and mother
and for family

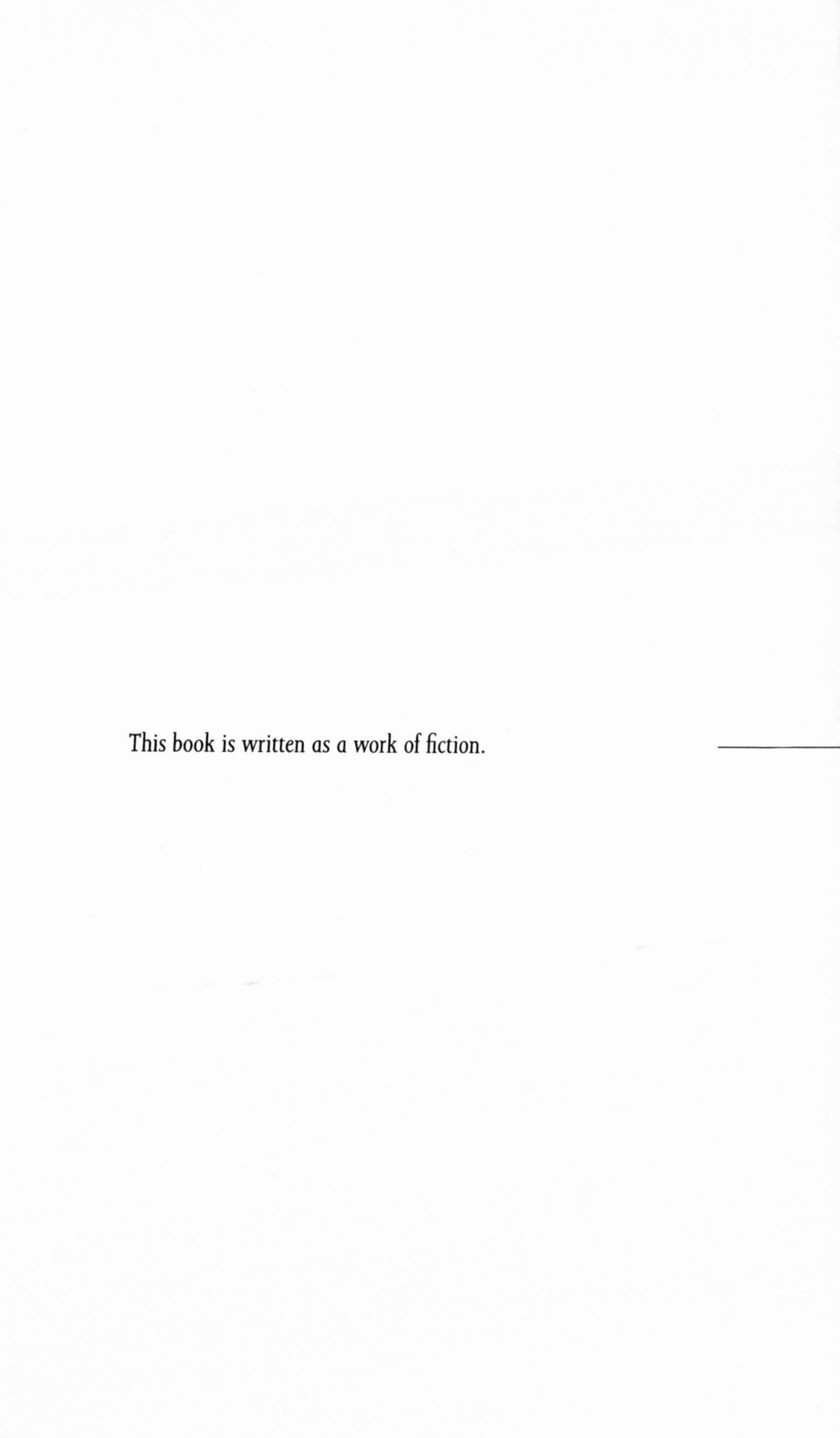

This book is written as a work of fiction.

We shall not cease from exploration
And the end of all our exploring
Will be to arrive where we started
And know the place for the first time.
—T. S. Eliot, "Little Gidding"

Contents

PART ONE

The Family Table

I

Under Grandma's dining room table it was dark and warm like the earth. The legs of the table were deep brown and thick. They were woven among one another, like the limbs of a jungle, leading everywhere and nowhere, within a circle. We played in them silently, timelessly.

The top of the table Grandma would have covered with a round tablecloth of white lace. She would set white, gold-rimmed cups and saucers around the circle, the cream and sugar in the center.

They would be seated around the table, drinking coffee and smoking cigarettes. The men wore khaki pants and wingtips, the women slim-fitting dresses and stockings and sleek shoes. They spoke intensely, in voices that rang with certainty and success. They were young, younger than we are now, and adult, more adult than we are now.

In the corner by the window, Grandma would sit and watch the afternoon Nevada snow fall quietly outside.

In the other corner, next to the blazing window of the stove, Grandpa would sit upright, straddling the oak straight-backed chair turned backwards.

Grandma would bring fresh coffee from the kitchen, and Grandpa would stand and add wood to the stove. The windows would steam up, and the room would fill with the smell of the coffee and the thick white cream, the smoke of the cigarettes, the warmth of the blazing stove.

In the dark of the underneath, the thick, interwoven legs of the table connected them. We could hear the pure, clear, crystalline ring of their voices. It sheltered, encircled the darkness, like a sphere.

2

In those days, Grandma was strong and sturdy, imposing. On Saturday, when they had left us for the weekend, she would be up early. We would awake to the smell of steaming chocolate, and bear claws warmed on the wood stove in the kitchen, lit hours before.

While we ate, Grandma would disappear into her bedroom. She would reappear in her elbow-sleeved dress made of black wool, looming above us, her hair braided neatly across the top of her head, wearing stockings and thick-heeled black shoes.

After we dressed, we would leave through the dark

entryway at the front of the U-shaped house. We would listen in vain for sounds of the small Indian family who rented the other side of the U, living silently in what was called the "apartment."

We would emerge from the screened front porch of the old white frame house, and would walk the chilled back-street sidewalks of Carson City. Grandma would wear her black purse over the forearm of her left coat sleeve, her chin high and her face turned forward, and we would proceed at a march to Main Street, then left one block to Gilbert's Drug.

Once arrived, Grandma would browse in the birthday card section and visit formally with the proprietor or his wife while we scanned the toy section, made our selection, and brought it to her. We would choose such morbid things as a rubber tarantula on a string, and once home we would choose the moment to dangle it in front of her. She would start with fright, then scowl furiously. Then she would smile in her twinkling, mischievous way as we paraded the spider, on its string, through the house in search of Grandpa.

In the afternoon she would sit by the corner window, working her crochet needles quickly and mechanically, producing more and more of the round lace doilies that ornamented the house. We would play in the back porch area outside the kitchen, the small area between the two wings of the house that trapped the afternoon sun. We crept slowly, silently in the direction of the woodpile, in ever futile attempts to seize one of the wild kittens that lived there. Grandma would bring warm milk in bowls, and we would crouch inside the kitchen door, waiting, as the kittens ever so tenuously appeared, and approached, and began to drink. Then we would emerge in a burst of glee, and in a split second the kittens would vanish. We knew they were in the woodpile, and were watching.

In the evening, after dinner, Grandma would dress for bed at the same time as we. She would emerge from her bedroom in her long robe, her braids taken down, draped behind her shoulders, down to her waist. We would stand by her chair in the window corner where the shade was pulled down now, and we would brush out her hair from the braids. It spread in silver, crimped waves down the front of her robe, more beautiful than anything we knew.

In the later evening, we would crawl into the double bed in the large far-back bedroom, and would shiver under the covers. Grandpa would come with wood, and he would light a fire in the small alabaster fireplace not far from the foot of our bed. Lying there, in the glow of the fire, we could hear the distant, quiet, enchanted sound of the old language that we did not understand and that was a part of this house. Later, over the quiet sound of the fire, we could hear Grandpa rattling in his attic bedroom above us, and the floorboards in Grandma's room next to us creak as she got into bed. At some moment, in the still, pure air of the bedroom and amidst the glow of the fire, we would cross over into sleep.

We would awake to Sunday morning sunlight, the alabaster fireplace cold, the smell of hot rum permeating the house. Grandma would seat us at the dining room table, at the white lace tablecloth. She would bring rolled pancakes soaked in a blend of maple syrup and rum. They had a taste that like the distant sound of the old language went only with this house. We ate them voraciously, gluttonously, searching for the sweet taste of the syrup.

Grandma would help us wash and dress in the bathroom, and send us to the dining room to wait. She would appear in her black wool dress, a black wool scarf tied around her head. She would hand a rosary to each of us.

We would walk the back streets to Saint Theresa's Catholic Church. We would ascend the steps, and once inside we would reach up, into the marble basin that held the holy water, and cross ourselves. We would proceed in Grandma's wake, taking a pew toward the front of the church, and kneeling, and crossing ourselves, and taking the rosary beads from our pockets. In the quiet before Mass had begun, we would bow our heads like Grandma, fingering the rosary beads and mimicking the silent movement of her lips. At some point we would break into muffled, uncontrollable laughter, and she would throw a black scowl that went through us.

She would proceed, whispering, with the infinite succession of rosaries that stretched right on through the Mass. Grandpa would arrive late, and would stand at the back, even when the church was half empty. He would vanish just after Communion, and afterwards we would find him waiting outside, on the sidewalk, outside the little wrought-iron fence that bordered the churchyard.

We would walk the back streets home, some up front with Grandpa, some at Grandma's side. It was like this time and time again.

3

On Christmas Day, the house would be transformed. The families would begin arriving in midafternoon, carrying packages. We would come through the gate in the front hedge, rattling the little wood address sign that hung on its front. We would come through the screen door and cross the old front porch. We would turn the brass knob on the heavy wooden door at the entrance and would flood into the dark, musty entryway. We would take an automatic sharp turn to the left, away from the wing where the Indians lived. We would proceed through an open door, and then make a sharp right into the long stretch of living room used only on this day. We would deposit the packages under the little Christmas tree that sat on a table in a bay window and proceed on past the couches and the oak rockers, past the old black baby grand whose top was a mass of family photographs. We would head through the white double doors that were opened up wide, into the noise of the dining room where family was everywhere: Grandma and Grandpa somewhere in the heat of the kitchen, aunts and uncles bustling from kitchen to dining room with martinis in hand, nineteen cousins crawling, toddling, darting every which way underfoot.

Later they would pull out a long folding table, setting its end against the old round dining room table, stretching it through the open double doors and down the length of the living room. Grandma would cover the entire length of the table with white tablecloths and would set the endless number of places. People would take seats all along the table, and Grandma would appear with steaming oval platters bearing the Christmas dinner. They poured red wine for all of us.

From where we sat along the stretch of table, we looked across to the photographs that covered the top of the baby grand. We ignored our own photographs, which were in color and were too recent, too familiar to have significance. We studied a brown-and-white print of a family of seven: the figure of the young, slender, delicately featured woman whose dark hair was braided neatly across the top of her head, the sculpted, dark-haired figure of the man seated next to her, the white-gowned infant held on his lap, the four other young children in obsolete clothes, all with the same round, deep brown eyes as the infant.

While we ate, Grandma would appear with ever more of the steaming platters. Grandpa would remain invisible, somewhere in the far corner of the kitchen, washing pots and pans.

Later, when the fresh coffee had been served up and the cigarettes lit, we would sneak safety pins from the middle drawer of a mission-style dresser in the dining room. We would creep quietly into the large, dark, far-back bedroom, and fully clothed, we would climb into the double bed. In the dark, we would pin our clothes to the sheets and then to each other's clothes. We would giggle quietly, ecstatically, with the thought that they would be unable to extricate us from the bed, that they would be forced to leave us there, together, until morning.

We would sleep amidst the distant ring of the voices, the distant clatter of more coffee being served up, unable to hear whether Grandpa had yet gone to his attic room above us.

4

This family in the brown-and-white print, the mother and the father and the five children with the round brown eyes, they were the immigrant story.

The father, of chiseled face and dark hair as thick as a horse's mane, and the mother, of delicate face and delicate body, of the dark braids wrapped about the head, they came from the green hills of the Basque Country of southern France, long before our own existences. They had come separately, fifteen years apart, crossing the Atlantic by ship and then the United States by train, he as a young sheepherder headed for the desert hills of the American West, she as a young woman hired to cook for a sheep ranch in western Nevada.

By the time they met, he had built his way up in a manner that could only be done in America, from lone herder to owner of a small band of sheep, to co-owner of a network of ranches that spanned eastern California and western Nevada. They married at Saint Thomas Aquinas Catholic Church in Reno, and a year later their first child, a boy, was born in a mansion on Reno's Court Street, high above the Truckee River. The mother would dress the infant in lace, and tuck him into a carriage fit for a king, and stroll on quiet afternoons through the parks that rimmed the river.

But then in the midst of the boy's first year the sheep market had plunged, and they lost everything to the banks. A second child arrived a year after the first, a boy also, born in a sheep camp outside of Alturas, California, in the desert hills where the father had found work as a herder. They lived in shacks and tents throughout eastern California and western Nevada, in country that was as harsh, as barren, as any you would want to know.

But when the boys were one and two, the mother herself seized on what it meant to be in America. She wrote home to the old farmhouse in the green hills, asking for the one hundred dollars that had been kept there for her, and two months later the money arrived. She took it and moved herself and the two baby boys into Carson City. She took a lease on a boarding house on Main Street, just across from the capitol grounds. She hired a girl to tend to the boys, and for eighteen hours a day she cooked and served and cleared and washed. The father would appear at intervals, tending bar until he became sick with cabin fever, then disappearing back into the hills.

Over the next eight years she bore three more children, all boys, standing over steaming kettles and dishpans until the moment the labor pains came, delivering the babies in the family quarters of the boarding house.

It was when the older boys were five and six that she made the decision to speak only English to them, and within a year they had lost all comprehension of the old Basque that their mother and father still spoke quietly to one another. She purchased the *Encyclopaedia Britannica* soon after the eldest started school, and then the works of Victor Hugo, translated. She sent the boys to roam in the room where Nevada's senators and judges drank and talked business over hot meals. In the end, all that the children had lost of the old Basque was made up for twice over in their command of the English language, because they knew the English of the books, and the English of the senators and judges, and the broken, accented English of their mother that had expressions no English-speaking person had ever uttered.

She raised them Catholic, in the church that was the link between this country and the green hills from which she came. Rain or snow or sun, at a quarter to seven on Sundays and on each of the forty days of Lent she could be seen parading the brood of five out the back door of the boarding house, along the back streets of Carson City, headed for Mass. One after the other the boys served their stints as altar boys and never lost their ability to recite the Latin liturgy.

When the older boys were twelve and thirteen, she took all that she had in savings and bought the U-shaped house, which came with full inventory of mission furniture, and bedding, and china and silver. She moved the five children into the first real home she had had since the mansion on Reno's Court Street, even if it meant that she would rise earlier, walking the back streets to the boarding house in pitch dark.

The father would come in work shirt and Levi's and laced walking boots, bearing the scent of the Nevada hills. He would sleep in the attic room at the top of the steep, narrow stretch of stairs that led up from the back porch. He would stay for two days, three at the most, then load his Ford pickup and disappear back into the hills.

As the mother's body lost its delicateness, as the father's face grew more and more weathered by sun and snow, the children shone with all that the father and the mother had hoped to find in this country, all that which was strong and young and unrestrained by a hundred generations of sameness. They flourished in school, in sports, in popularity, increasingly with each progression from grade school toward high school. And then onward, the boys one by one heading for a Jesuit university in California, the income from the boarding house making its way unfailingly to the school's office for tuition and fees. The children learned things, saw things, knew things that went light years beyond what their parents had any hope of knowing.

This, from the green hills to the university degrees,

we grew up knowing like a catechism, never formally instructed, but acquired in bits and pieces that we seized on and held in our minds with solemnity. We knew too that at the heart of the story was the dining room table, the table that was round and made of dark wood and lace-covered, the table where early on the children of immigrants had formed a circle that protected them, that strengthened them, that over time had become a place of privilege, where only family was allowed.

5

In our own house in Reno, in our family of five, it was a world apart from the U-shaped house in Carson, and yet somehow connected with it.

For the three of us children, our earliest memory was of the sound of the typewriter, because it was there always, in the early morning hours as we woke, in the late night as we slept, in the background as we played. It had its own rhythm: a steady, continuous rap . . . then a slower rap . . . then a stalling, uneven rap . . . then silence . . . then an endless silence . . . then explosion into a flurry of sound . . . then quiet again.

It came from the charcoal black Royal typewriter that sat on our father's desk in a far corner of the house, and it was the same typewriter, and the same distant sound, during all of our growing up years.

We were six and four and two the day when in mid-afternoon our mother sat us on the front step of our little subdivision house in Reno, and our father rushed home early from his work at the university, and we drank champagne, there on the front step, the five of us. The words *book contract* and *Harper* and *New York agent* became fused with the warmth of the afternoon and the way time seemed to have come to a halt. We sat there on the cement step, the five of us, in our own impenetrable circle of celebration.

Then one evening our father's brothers came to our house and sat on the couches in our living room and listened as one of them read aloud the chapters that had been written thus far. They listened closely, with expressions of intelligence on their faces. At the end there was a silence, our father even more somber and tense than he had been throughout the reading. Then came the words of approval, and the exhaling, our father's face taking on a glow, a radiance, the room filling with the air of celebration.

When we were a year older, our father handed to each of us that which you could actually hold, a little book that had form and weight, that was deep blue in color, to each our own copy inscribed separately.

Even before we were old enough to read, we knew what the book was about. We knew that it was about our grandfather, about a trip our father had made with him back to the green hills of the old country, after a lifetime in the desolation of the Nevada desert. We knew that it had to do with the beauty of the green hills, but somehow, too, with the strange, rugged beauty of the desert hills and of the man who had grown old in them. We knew that it had to do with our father, too, that it had to do with his own voyage of discovery, of his father, of the gentle beauty of the distant land from which all of us had sprung.

The deep blue book was that which each of us, if ever a fire had struck our house, would have taken first.

6

Our father, who was the second-born, was most devoted to his elder brother. We knew this from things that were never said, like the innumerable times that the telephone rang and our father said, "If it's for me I've gone to Tahiti," and then on being informed that the caller was his elder brother, said unhesitatingly, "I'll pick it up in the bedroom." We knew it from the way we would pack up and drive to Carson unfailingly when invited to his elder brother's house, even if it meant that other commitments had to be canceled. We knew it from the way our father would change demeanor when in the company of his brother, his face taking on a look of strength and peace and promise.

People would say that the two of them were so alike and yet so different, and this was true. Of all of the five, they had the round, deep brown eyes that were the most indistinguishable. They had hands that were indistinguishable, strong hands with defined bones and pronounced knuckles. They had frames that were the same, too, just under six feet, square-shouldered and of medium weight, and they sat the same way, one foot to the ground and the other crossed over, squarelike. They each had the familial good skin that tanned the color of rawhide in summer.

And yet in ways equally fundamental they were as different as night and day. Our father, named Anthony, was quiet and craved privacy, and it was for this reason that he, of all the brothers, had chosen to live at arm's distance from Carson. In the face of his family's skepticism he had followed a career as a writer. He had married our mother, a fair-haired beauty who had a love for the arts. He had forged himself a position as director of a fledgling press at the University of Nevada in Reno, and bought a modest house in a new subdivision on the edge of town. On weekends he took his wife and children shooting in the foothills west of town, and he loved his dog, a male collie with fur the color of autumn. His closest friends were a cowboy artist-professor from Oklahoma who had ridden the bulls in Madison Square Garden, and a fiction writer, nationally known, twenty years his senior. He sang *Clementine*, *Home on the Range*, and *My Old Kentucky Home* to his children at night. And his family ate dinner by candlelight.

His elder brother, named Luke, was the first to have taken the path to law school. He had married the daughter of a Carson City attorney, and after law school had returned to his hometown. He was a good young lawyer and prospered. To the west of Carson he built a hundred-thousand-dollar home where there were people coming and going at all times of the day: strangers emerging from the guest bedroom at nine in the morning, vaguely familiar faces helping themselves in the kitchen, Indian girls folding laundry and serving up sandwiches, people standing with drinks in hand at the pool table, more people lounging by the swimming pool as the six children arrived home from school. There were parties where the entire grounds were lit up and the children and their cousins ran wild until one in the morning, where our uncle moved through the crowd with a warmth, with a confidence, that seemed to infect people.

Our father said it so many times that we had no memory of the first time, how such and such a person had remarked that our uncle was prime material for *political office*. We knew the term long before we had any idea of what it meant, except that we knew it had to do with the difference between our father and his brother.

But for us, it was the sameness that prevailed over the difference, because we felt the same in each of their laps. It was a sense of something that went far back, long before our own existences, somehow connected with the old country, with green hills and dark earth.

7

If our father and his elder brother were a paradox of sameness and difference, so too was the third brother, named Mitchell, an enigma of likeness and unlikeness to our grandfather. He had the height of our grandfather, and an identical face, chiseled and strong-jawed. He had the hair of the young father in the brown-and-white print, black, and thick as a horse's mane.

Of the five of them, he was the second to have taken the path to law school, following the steps of the eldest brother but then veering off on an altogether separate path. He lived the life of a bachelor, a life apart from us and of which we knew little, relocating time and time again to new jobs and to apartments no one ever saw. In this too there was something of our grandfather in him, appearing and then disappearing from the U-shaped house.

But in a sense far more fundamental, he was the opposite of our grandfather. And it was this which shone in his face as he appeared at the U-shaped house, the expression that like the others' seemed to change as he crossed through the double doors into the dining room. It was as though he came there for sustenance, to refuel and rekindle. And in this he was as different from our grandfather as night from day.

8

Just as our father and his older brother bore the scent of the old country, the two youngest of them were infused with the light of the new world.

In the fourth-born, named Mark, it was a lightness of heart that found its place in his smile, the smile that shone from the face of the two-year-old in the brown-and-white print, the smile that was pure sun. At the Jesuit university he had married a girl of Italian descent, and on returning he had followed a career as a history teacher at Carson City's high school. They had five children, one after the next, who had the sunlit smile and the sweetness of heart from which it came. The bunch of them would come bounding out of their station wagon onto the sidewalk in front of the U-shaped house, carrying ribbon-tied packages from the bakeries of Carson. As they burst into the house it was as if the shades were being opened up room by room, setting the house aglow.

And then Francis, the baby of the five, of the same round brown eyes but of more delicate build, whose mind bore the light of the new world. Since childhood they had said he was the one who would outshine them all, the one who had gone on to graduate *maxima cum laude* from the Jesuit university in California, the one whose books filled the old mission bookcase that lined the back wall of the entryway to Grandma's house. He had married a young woman who was as delicate in face and body as a porcelain doll, and his five children were the youngest, and the best dressed, and the most Catholic of us all.

In our earliest years he was completing that which our father called the "doctoral degree in English literature," teaching high school in Carson while writing that which our father called a *brilliant dissertation*. He would come through the double doors of the dining room, and behind his black-rimmed glasses there was a look of intelligence in his eyes, pure and analytical, safeguarded from emotion.

Then suddenly he had changed paths, he had taken his family and headed for law school in the wake of our eldest and middle uncles. He had returned for the summers to work for Uncle Luke, and at the end of three years had returned permanently. Our father said it over and over again, how he had the golden mind, how he of all of them could have chosen any path and have shone.

9

The nineteen of us, we had the good skin that tanned dark in summer. We had the eyes. We had the same rosaries from Grandma. We knew the music of the old language that we did not understand, we had eaten the same pancakes soaked in syrup and rum. We had the same dark playground under Grandma's dining room table, we had the same burning desire to catch the kittens that lived in the woodpile. We had the same connection to the mother and the father and the five children in the brown-and-white print. We had the same connection to the deep blue book that told our grandfather's story, we had the same link to the old earth and green hills from which our grandparents had come. We had the same blood.

10

In the quiet of Grandma's bedroom, against the ring of the dining room, and the small group of us there around the bed. And the old dark rosaries that hung from the bedpost, and the warm scent of Grandma that filled the quiet of the room. And the sun-darkened limbs of Uncle Francis's fifth-born. The dark limbs reaching, touching the rosaries and rattling them. And the face of him who was the most beautiful of us, round-eyed, brown-eyed, good-skinned, angelic. Freshly diapered, at play, and the dance of the rosaries in the quiet of Grandma's room. The sun-darkened limbs beside the white of his mother's dress, against the pure white cotton dress. And the young mother resting, there on the bed beside the child against the crystalline ring of the dining room.

Angelic, this one was. And the group of us hovering there. He was our favorite. He was all that was good in us.

11

In spring, we would make the hour's drive south twenty miles past Carson, then southeast through the little town of Wellington, pulling off the highway at mid-morning and heading down the straight strip of dirt road that led to one of the sheep ranches. We would find our grandfather there in the corrals, amidst the dust and the ewes and the new lambs.

He would take one of us up in one arm and a new lamb in the other, and standing there in his dust-covered Levi's and brown denim work shirt and round-toed work boots, his sun-darkened face and snow-white hair framed against the clear blue of the Nevada sky, he would break into a smile that was as radiant, as pure, as the spring sun.

In the warmth of the late morning, he would bottle feed milk to the bummer lambs, those whose mothers had died or rejected them, and they would take it in one swoosh, filling the bottle with foam.

We could smell the dust and the warmth of the Nevada desert, and the sun-cracked wood of the corral posts and the denim of our grandfather's work shirt, mixed in with the bleating of the newborns, with the sight of the snow-white wool and the spatterings of blood and the clear, clear blue of the Nevada sky.

12

At other times we would walk with Grandpa into a canyon that lay in the foothills of the Sierra just west of Carson, that smelled of sun-warmed sage and pine in fall, fresh snow and cold pine in winter. It had a wide, sagebrush-covered promontory that our father and mother dubbed the "peninsula," and a steep forest of straight pines that rose up just where the dirt road crossed the back of the peninsula. A wide band of aspen ran along the side of the peninsula and on up into the heart of the forest, following the path of a freshwater creek that wound down from the mountains beginning with the first snows. By late October the creek bed would be dry, its fine sand twinkling with specks of fool's gold. And the band of aspen would have turned, it stretched like a blaze of light up the depth of the canyon. It was family land.

Grandpa was like a young deer there. He knew the land, every inch of it; he knew the road in and the best place to leave the pickup and the best path across the peninsula, the place to be on the alert for rattlesnakes, the exact degree of coldness at which you no longer needed to watch for rattlers. He knew the best path up into the heart of the forest, and the best spot to stop and break out the picnic lunch, and the best spot for Christmas trees this year. He was like a solitary young deer that welcomed the company of our visit, that beamed with pride as he stooped and seized a piece of petrified wood and handed it to us. But at the same time like the young deer he would bound up the mountain free of us, disappearing from us, and with our father and mother we would follow with our slow, laboring steps.

It was what our father had written in the deep blue book. Our grandfather was at home here, his soul did not reside in any house, it could not be kept in any house, it was part of the land, it was one with the snow and the pines and the sage and the autumn blaze.

13

On a morning in July would be the gathering at the gate, just past the junction at Spooner Summit on the road from Carson City to Lake Tahoe. The cars would pull off the highway into the dirt area just outside the gate. Our father would call out that our grandfather had buried the key just to the side of the right gatepost, and then the horde of us would emerge from the cars and begin the search. One time we dug up the entirety of the right hillside, and then the left for the possibility that our father was mistaken, without finding the key to the padlock. We ate lunch sitting cross-legged all over the road inside the gate, the parents and aunts and uncles mumbling under their breath that one of these days we had better get some duplicates of the goddamned key made.

But at other times the key was found just where it was supposed to be, and the gate was swung open, the cars heading through in a cloud of dust, those in the last car stopping and locking the gate behind us. Then time would stand still, the caravan heading in, winding its way from the hum of the highway, silence descending inside the cars. We passed a quiet meadow lake, taking the left fork at its far end, and then a gentle slope upwards. We headed through pines that were tall and straight and so thick that the sun broke through only in threads of light, and then we broke onto a clearing, a grass meadow crisscrossed by streams, rich with wildflowers. We passed an old abandoned cabin that sat on the edge of the meadow, and then we began the steeper climb, through more of the straight pines and then into the aspen, past the grey-white trunks that bore the initials of sheepherders long dead, through the dance of the sun on the quaking leaves. And then upwards, out of the aspen grove, the road riding a high ridge until it broke onto a high valley floor covered with streams, specked by wildflowers pale in color now, rimmed on the far side by mountains more massive, more bare, than we had ever known. Then the first snowflowers, one or two at the most, bright red against the patches of snow here and there beside the road. Then upwards from the far side of the valley floor into a forest of gnarled, twisted pines, the road ragged from fallen trees. We listened to the hum of the car and breathed the air that was pure and cold now.

At the moment we broke the ridge and looked down on the hidden lake, deep blue, glimmering, it was a spell broken. Inside the cars was the sound of deep breaths being let out, and then the yipping began. The caravan plowed downward, descending to the rim of the lake and veering to the right, the sunlit blue of the lake visible through the aspen, the road following the rim of the lake and then heading upwards, away from the lake.

At the crest on the far side of the lake was a flat, sandy area called the *lookout*, where the cars would pull off the road and the doors would open up and we would come piling out. In the chill of the high mountain air we would button our coats up to our chins, and we would stand with them, looking down on the deep blue lake and outward, beyond it, a thousand feet below it, to the gentle, pale blue expanse of Tahoe, maternal, rimmed by mountains so distant they were purple in color, the whole earth stretching out below the clear, sun-filled blue of the Nevada sky.

We would pile back into the cars and head onward, taking a left fork and curving around a last, sandy hill. And from there we looked down on that place tucked deep in these mountains that was our grandfather's summer camp, that place that like the canyon in the foothills was *family land*. We could see from afar the shape of the canvas tent. We could see the shape of the huge stock truck that had made it in fifteen years before and was not expected to ever make it back out again, and we could see our grandfather's pickup, faded green. We could see the little stacks of wood that would supply each of the families for winter, and in the distance we could see the small band of sheep that he would have taken to the high mountains for summer. We could see the shape of our grandfather, his right arm waving, his snow-white hair blowing in the mountain air.

In the night, the campfire aglow, they would pile us into the canvas-topped bed of the huge old stock truck, innumerable cousins placed every which way under blankets. We would lie in the dark and look out the open back end of the truck to a sky so laden with stars that at places they seemed to be blended together. Against the distant ring of the voices that surrounded the campfire, we could smell the dust and the gnarled pines, and we could feel the cold mountain air on our faces and the warmth of each other's small bodies that filled the bed of the truck. We knew that this place, hidden deep in the high mountains, like the other things, was in our blood.

In the morning, our mothers would cook bacon and eggs over the pit that Grandpa would have rimmed with fresh white rocks just for this visit, and make hot chocolate from canned Carnation milk, and we would romp in the sand and on the rocks that surrounded the camp.

In mid-afternoon, dust-covered and sunbaked, we would pile into the cars, and the caravan would head out again, leaving Grandpa alone with the wood and the small band of sheep and the chill breeze that blew quietly through the camp. We would roll out slowly, passing the lookout and heading down through the aspen that rimmed the lake, veering up away from the lake and over the ridge, descending through the forest of gnarled pines, crossing the high valley floor, moving down the high ridge and through the aspen grove, down through the straight pines and out past the old cabin and the meadow, past the meadow lake, to the place where the dirt road led back to the gate. The driver of the last car would emerge, and head up to the gate and swing it open, the caravan moving back onto the highway.

Then the drive down the highway that led back to Carson, and the regathering at the U-shaped house, Grandma in the swing on the screened front porch, aproned, standing to greet the boisterous crowd that smelled of dust and pine.

Then the quiet half-hour at the dining room table, and the smell of the fresh coffee and the thick white cream and the smoke of the cigarettes, and the sound of the voices that surrounded the underneath.

14

We had no word for it, and yet it was always there, at the heart of everything they said and in the very tones in which they spoke. It was what made their faces change when they came together, it was that which made the circle hold.

It had to do with something infinitely old, that went back to the dark earth that bore our grandparents, and their grandparents for ten thousand years back, something that bound the circle back to the old earth. And yet, too, it had something new and enlightened to it, like the gold rimming on Grandma's coffee cups.

It was there always, at the soul of the creature called family, unconditional, unquestioned. It was that which, from the dark underneath of Grandma's white-laced table, made their voices ring purely. It was that which lingered at the center of the table, atop the white lace, at the very place where the cream and sugar sat.

The Citadel

I

It was raining the afternoon in early October when our Volkswagen squareback, sparkling new and bearing a USA plaque on its back, came over the last ridge, and we looked down into the valley that held the little village of Saint-Jean-Pied-de-Port. We were groaning and shielding our ears from the excruciating screech of the wipers as they crossed the windshield, and my father, condemned to endure the sound, was clutching the wheel and peering out through the rain, ready to commit mayhem. But as we cleared the last ridge all of the tension in the car suddenly lifted, and the rain stopped, and we pulled off the road and looked down into the valley. We looked onto the gentle, green hills where the mist rose up and floated and spread in waves over the velvet green. We looked onto the little grey stone village and the church tower rising up in the center and the little river that wound its way through the village, and looking across the valley, high above the village, we saw the massive stone fortress that reigned over the valley, the autumn forest that spread out beneath it, the great stone wall that rimmed it and wound its way downward, encircling the inner core of the village. We got out of the car and stood by the side of the curve in the road, in silence.

From the ridge in the late afternoon, we could see the yellow lights already burning in the maze of interconnected stone houses of the inner core of the village and in the scatterings of little two-story white houses, all with red-tile roofs and red shutters, that lay on the outskirts outside of the stone wall. We could see the little roads that wound their way out of the village, and the old farmhouses scattered along them, and the small bands of sheep, white against the green hillsides. We could smell the steam rising up from the ground, laden with the sweet, drenched scent of grass and earth and fallen leaves.

2

We had the blood of these green hills in us. I almost twelve, and my brother fourteen and my sister nine, we had the good skin and the eyes and now our hair too, the flaxen color from our mother, was in the midst of turning. And our father too, he had the blood of these green hills in him, and he had come back to them, he would write of them.

The five of us, we had left at the time that was our last chance for calm before the flurry that had already begun to gather itself. Uncle Luke ready to announce for the governor's race that would come one year from this fall, and the look of pride-mixed-with-hesitation that had come into my father's eyes. And in the heat of August, the huge black trunks that were Grandma's had been set out in the driveway of our little subdivision house in Reno, and packed as if for a trip to Siberia. We had packed them full of Theragran vitamins and Crest toothpaste and Bayer aspirin, and Beatles magazines and surfer shirts, and the articles of feminine hygiene that my mother said I might be needing before the year was out, and all else that was genuine America.

We had closed them and locked them and shipped them, and then one month later we had followed in their path, the five of us, toting suitcases and the charcoal black Royal out onto the Reno runway on a morning in late September. And even as we settled into the seats of the airplane, even as we listened to the first sound of the propellers, the new look had seemed to begin to fade from our father's eyes.

And now, as we stood on the ridge in late afternoon and looked down into the green valley, it had vanished entirely.

3

The rhythm of the Royal, it had traveled with us, silent inside the charcoal black case, and now on the first night it started up again, the faint, distant, familiar sound. It wound its way through the ground floor of the house and upwards to the rooms where we slept, deep into the late hours of the night, mixing with the sweet, drenched scent of the valley.

There was something in the name of the house that was related to the sound of the typewriter, as though by some strange reversal of sequence the house had been built for us, conceived for us, years before the day when we would arrive here. The house sat on the outskirts on the far side of the village, on the edge of a wide field that bordered the river, alone, not part of the little clusters into which the other houses of the valley were grouped. It rose up four stories high, larger than any other house in the valley, and yet its style was identical to that of the other houses, traditional, of white plaster and red tile and the heavy wooden shutters painted red.

It had been built by a Basque businessman who was a native of this village, who had departed in his youth and had found fortune in business dealings in South America. Still in his fifties he had made plans to return here and had built the house on the outskirts. But for some reason he had never returned, and the house had sat vacant for the five years before our arrival.

Inside, it was the same blend of the old and the new, the same blend of something that did and did not fit in this valley, so curious that our mother always said that the house made you feel as if you were in the old country and at home at the same time. There was a huge kitchen with gas stove and no dishwasher, and a long, wood-floored dining room with a table that could easily seat sixteen. It had innumerable toilets, like Uncle Luke's house in Carson City, and yet the toilets were located in small, closetlike places separate from the bathrooms that had tub and sink and *bidet*. On the ground floor, just inside the entrance where Grandma's huge black trunks stood upright, was what was called the *salon*, a small room carpeted wall-to-wall, with built-in bookcases and firm couches and an American-style coffee table. There was a study for our father to work in, with a desk of dark wood, on the ground floor just next to the *salon*.

The name of the house was like the house itself, because it was there painted in red in the traditional way on the white plaster gatepost to the right of the red gate at the front. And yet it was different, unlike the other house names, which were for families or wives or mothers or daughters. The name of the house was *Goizean Goiz*, the name that our father said meant *early in the morning* in Basque. The name had a translucence to it; it had the clean, pure, untouched first light of dawn to it.

And the faint, distant rhythm of the Royal, it blended with the name in the same way that it blended with the sweet, drenched scent of the afternoon rain that floated through the dark upstairs of the house. Into the deep hours of the night, it was as though the house was being anointed with our presence.

4

Sunday morning, the sun shining all over the valley, a sparkling sunlight that drew the steam up from the green hills. We drove to the village square, and parked, and walked the cobblestone street to the entrance of the church. There were massive double doors opened up wide, and there the people of the village turned their heads and stared.

My father and my older brother veered left, disappearing up a dark, narrow stairway. We walked onto the cold, stone floor of the church and took a place amidst the rows of wicker pews. We looked at the faces of the women kneeling all around us, women with the delicate face at all stages of life, the radiant face of youth and the cragged face of old age alike encircled by the same scarf of thick black wool. We looked up to the dark wood balcony that surrounded the inside of the church on all except the altar side and saw the row of men in black berets, kneeling at the rail. On the floor of the church we saw the women's rosaries come out and watched the lips move inaudibly, and then we heard the singing that was so pure it took your breath away. We saw the priest emerge and heard the familiar words of the Latin begin, winding out through the pews and up through the balcony. We saw the row of men in the balcony quietly begin to shuffle out just after Communion and heard the bells ring out into the village as Mass was ended.

5

Two kilometers from the village core, the little road sunlit, old women in black making way for the Volkswagen squareback, sparkling new. The path into the front yard, the frantic clucking of the chickens that roamed it. The little motor of the Volkswagen turned off, and the doors opened up. The farmhouse bathed in sunlight. The imprint in the old stone that was part of the wall of the farmhouse, ancient, familiar, and foreign at once. Recognizable and unrecognizable at once, part of the wall of the farmhouse, the name that we bore.

The old woman in black appearing in the dark space

of the doorway, then emerging, embracing us on one cheek and then the other. Leading us into the dark space of the doorway. The dark, musty, earthen-floored smell of the inside. The open doorway to the right, and the long, narrow dining room filled with sunlight. The long, rectangular table that stretched nearly the length of the room. The red tablecloth embroidered in green, and stoneware dishes, and bottles of red wine.

Then slowly, the faces emerging from the door that must have led to the kitchen, the face of a man in black beret who looked strangely like my father, the face of a woman, raven-haired, the faces of children roughly our own ages, dark-haired, all with the same eyes as our own. Emerging one by one, quietly, with a reticence by which they seemed to blend into the farmhouse. Each pronouncing beneath his breath a word of greeting that we did not understand, looking down as they approached and embraced us on each cheek.

The three of us mute at the table through the endless afternoon, against the hum of the quiet, halting conversation that we could not understand. The courses of food that were so many we had lost count: first the soup and the bread, then the chicken, then the mutton, then the fish, then the salad, then cheese, then for the adults the interminable coffee and brandy and cigarettes.

The little motor of the Volkswagen starting back up at seven in the evening, the three of us from the back seat complaining of the agony of the afternoon. Our parents amused, speaking of how the family had probably worked for a week preparing that meal. Speaking of how it was the event of a decade for American cousins to have appeared at the door of the farmhouse. Then our parents' voices turning more serious, against the hum of the little motor of the Volkswagen. Speaking of that which we already knew. They spoke of heritage. They spoke of the blood of the green hills, they spoke of the farmhouse and the faces and the hundred generations of sameness.

6

It was named *La Citadel*, the massive stone fortress that spread across the hill above the village, reigning over the village and the green valley. Built at the time of the Roman occupation and then fortified over the centuries, used for military purposes as recently as World War II, it was now the village's *école publique*. Our father said over and over again how envious he was. It was like stepping back through the centuries, he said, and if ever any of us were to become writers, this would be the thing to write about.

The three of us whose hair was in the midst of turning, we were dressed in *tabliers*, smocks made of crisp white cotton that kept our clothes clean underneath. We carried briefcases called *cartables*, filled with pens called *stilos* and notebooks called *cahiers* and erasers called *gommes*. Early in an overcast morning that bore the scent of the green hills, our father and mother alongside us, we walked the lane that led toward the village. At a crest in the lane we took a left fork, heading up away from the village, into the oak forest of the Citadel. In the air was the smell of the dark wet earth of the forest, mixed in with the smell of the autumn leaves beneath our feet.

At the top the road came out of the forest, emerging onto an expanse of green grass, then led to a stone drawbridge over a waterless, grass-covered moat. We crossed over the drawbridge and headed through stone walls that were forty feet high, entering a vast, stone-floored inner courtyard that was encircled by buildings.

The courtyard was laced with children in the white *tabliers*, alive with them, some darting in all directions beneath an airborne soccer ball, some standing in groups, and their chatter filled the morning air. Slowly the chatter grew quieter and quieter as the groups in the white *tabliers* turned one by one to look at us. By the time we reached the center of the courtyard you could hear our footsteps on the stone floor. Then, as we proceeded in the direction of a sign that read *Directrice*, a quiet murmur started up and then grew louder and louder, filling the courtyard. We headed into the building at the far end of the courtyard, and on entering we heard the sound of a buzzer, and then, instantly, there was quiet in the courtyard.

It was midmorning by the time they led us out of the building, each in a separate direction across the courtyard. Our mother, who had studied French at the university and had a better command of it than our father, had done all of the talking. She had produced our passports and our last report cards from home, and had seemed to be attempting to explain the significance of American As and Bs. A stout, serious woman in a white *tablier* just like our own had pulled from her desk a series of papers that read *Fiche d'Inscription* across the top, and our mother had sat for an hour filling them out. Then the woman had stepped out of the office and returned with three boys who looked too old to be students here, who wore the same *tablier* but royal blue in color. The woman pointed to them, saying, "Conseiller! Conseiller!" and our parents, looking relieved to be on their way, said, "Okay, have a great first day." *Cartables* in hand, we followed the *conseillers* out of the building and into the courtyard, heading each to a different little door in the buildings that rimmed it.

You could feel the chill in the stone building as soon as we entered it and in the dim light headed onto the wood stairs. At the top of the flight of stairs there was a closed door, and behind it I could hear the voice of a woman, and then the voice of a girl. The *conseiller* knocked quietly at the door and then opened it, and I could see the woman who was standing there, thin and erect, her hair rolled tightly at the back of her head. She was holding a wooden pointer, and pointing it to a moveable blackboard that stood beside her. She turned silent and lowered the pointer as we crossed the thresh-hold, and without even looking in the direction of the class I could see the mass of white *tabliers* and could feel the mass of dark eyes fixed on me. I stood at the front of the class in my new *tablier*, my *cartable* in hand, peering out through my Rolling Stone bangs across to the window that lent onto the courtyard.

The *conseiller* spoke quietly to the woman at the front of the class and then headed back out the door, closing it without a sound. The woman said something aloud, and then I realized she was saying it to me. I looked at her, and then she said it again, the short sentence that was so palpable that I could have reached out and grabbed it, the sentence that was grey in color and had no meaning. I stood there at the front of the class, and the woman began to glare at me. And then suddenly it came to me, the sentence with which our mother had prearmed us, and I said it aloud, "Je ne comprends pas," looking right at her.

There was a muffled giggle from somewhere among the rows of white *tabliers*, and the woman grabbed the wooden pointer and struck the desk with it. She put the pointer back down on the desk, stepped toward me and took my arm, and led me slowly, as one would lead an ignorant beast or a blind person, to an open desk in the back row of the class. She resumed her place at the front of the class, and took up the pointer again. She pointed it to a spot on the moveable blackboard that said *le point*, and then to a straight line labeled *la ligne*.

She started with a whole stream of the grey-colored language that, as I sat there mute in the back row, blended in with the empty courtyard and overcast sky that were visible through the window. I could see the profiles of the girls in the row in front of me, the delicate faces with short-cropped hair as dark as a raven, every one of them with pierced ears and little earrings of pure gold.

There was something about the morning that like the name imprinted in the old stone I recognized and yet did not recognize, something old and familiar, and strange and new at the same time, the romance of the Citadel and the beauty of the tiny gold earrings all mixed in with the massiveness of the Citadel and the sickening greyness of the classroom.

7

Autumn, and we knew the smells of the Citadel, that on the first day were new and thick and palpable like the language.

There was the smell of the oak forest, the smell of the dark earth and fallen red leaves, wet and rich in the morning rain. The clean, starched scent of the *tabliers* in morning, over the navy blue clothes worn underneath. The grey, nauseous smell of the classroom. The smell of the noon meal, of steaming chicken and fresh bread, of the spray of the oranges, mistlike, as the peel was pulled away. The stench that emanated from the w.c. just behind the buildings surrounding the courtyard, that permeated the air inside the stalls. The smell in the earthen-floored *vestibule* lined with clothes hooks, the strange, new acrid smell of old sweat that came out from under the white *tabliers* and filled the room as we changed into shorts for *gymnastique*. The green scent of the old moat covered with grass, where we were split into *équipes* and learned to play soccer.

And the episodes that were fused with the smells, inseparable.

The afternoon on the second day of school, when the girl who sat next to me in class approached the spot where I stood in the courtyard, and told me her name, Beatrice, and stood there with me, and then at the buzzer walked with me back up the stairs to class, and took her seat next to me. The teacher started up in the thick grey language, and the mass of children in the white *tabliers* took out paper and pen and began to write. Like a little mother determined that I would learn, the girl named Beatrice slid her paper to the side of her desk, whispering, "Copie! Copie!" Letter by letter, I copied from her beautiful hand the word *Dictée* at the top, and then the words that made the first paragraph. Then came the explosion, the teacher marching toward us, taking my paper and ripping it in two, speaking the grey language in a piercing tone to Beatrice, who hung her head, while the mass of the white *tabliers* turned and stared.

There had been the episode in the infirmary, just next to the office of the *Directrice*, on the morning of the *examen physique*. There were two nurses, in white smocks almost identical to our own *tabliers*, and one of them placed a stethoscope on my chest and pronounced, "Toussez!" Into the chill, crisp air of the infirmary I began to whistle, first at a moderate-volume monotone. The nurse with the stethoscope stared in bewilderment, and then she coughed in a retching way, as though she had something caught in her throat. Then again she pronounced, "Toussez! Toussez!" and I let forth a splendid whistling tune that I invented on the spot. The air of the infirmary was then filled with the nurses' uncontrolled laughter, and then they threw up their hands and sent me away.

There had been the late afternoon after *gymnastique* was ended, when I was the last in the girl's earthen-floored *vestibule*, standing there in my slip called a *combinaison* that I had bought with my mother at a shop just off the village square only a few days before, that in my mind I could not disentangle from the word *communion* and the image of the sacred host and the ringing of the bells at Mass. Like an apparition, the group of boys appeared in the doorway which had no door, silhouetted against the sunlight of the outside. They stood there staring, in the light of the doorway, while I fumbled frantically, struggling first into my dress and then into my *tablier*. And then silent, they divided at the doorway as, *cartable* in hand, I forged my way out, carrying with me all in one bundle the image of the *combinaison* and the sacred host and the ringing of the bells and the acrid smell of the *vestibule*.

And the uneventful afternoon when *gymnastique* was held on the *esplanade*, the wide, flat expanse of green that lay outside the back wall of the Citadel, on a plateau looking out over the next valley. In the mid-autumn afternoon, the gentle Basque sun had shone down all over the esplanade, drying the grass and warming it. From the place where the soccer ball flew, you could see the splendor of the fortress against the pale blue sky that spread out above the valleys, and you were bathing in the gentle autumn sun of two thousand years ago, and for that instant and from that view the Citadel was a place of beauty untarnished.

8

Late autumn, and our father with a stack of typewritten pages a half-inch thick by now. He would walk through the forest of the Citadel in early morning, returning to the house named *Goizean Goiz* and sitting down to his typewriter and working through the day. We would cross the threshhold at that certain moment at the end of each school day, and the sound of the English language, clean and lucid and full of meaning, would ring out over the distant tapping of the old Royal. The house was a little fortress, our mother said. We were coming to know the meaning of family in a new way.

And the sphere that was taking form there in the inside of me. The sphere forming around the visions from home, the old visions mixed in with the new visions borne on the wings of the letters that took four weeks to arrive. The smell of the dust and sage and pine, and the gleam of the deep blue lake, and the view from the *lookout*, the color of aspen in fall, and Grandpa bounding, and Grandma aproned, all mixed in with the first junior high school dance in October when the boys were actually kissing the girls, and the thrill of hullabaloo boots and fishnet stockings and how *Seventeen* magazine was all the rage. The sphere forming there in the inside of me and sitting with me amidst the grey language, separate. Even the smells of the Citadel could not reach it.

9

Autumn moving into the wet, chill Basque winter, and the three of us having begun to penetrate the grey language. Having dared to speak. We had *cahiers* that were actually written in, in a hand that was smooth and regular and upright and looked nothing like our handwriting at home. We made our ones almost like American sevens, and crossed our sevens, and opened our *ps*, and set up our division computations in the new way in which the quotient appeared miraculously with nothing under it, and you could proceed on, adding to it or subtracting from it or multiplying it or dividing it.

And the girl Beatrice, raven-haired, gold-earringed. She who since that early day of the torn *dictée* had been a little mother to me, she who had been silently aware since the first day of every move I made in class, of each word I uttered aloud in the courtyard. There at her desk, or amidst the group of girls we mixed with in the courtyard, in her starched *tablier* and short-cropped hair and tiny gold earrings, she had a poker face, baby-faced and round-eyed, unnoticing and unfazed, the best

I have ever seen except for one. Only later, when we were alone in a far corner of the courtyard, would the baby face transform, taking on a look of concern, the look of the mother, quietly instructing me on the error I had made aloud in class, quietly instructing me as to why the group of girls in the courtyard had just now broken into muffled laughter.

She told me things that she did not speak of to the other girls, as if she knew that the things she said could not come back to haunt her, because at the end of the school year I and the things she said would be leaving, disappearing back out from the green valley and the village and the Citadel where next year she would be proceeding on to *cinquième*. She talked of her disdain for the teacher and for school itself, how if she had her choice she would stay home at the farm, spending the days with her father in the fields, speaking only Basque. She talked of the group of boys that stood in the far corner of the courtyard just inside the huge open doors, who were *sales* and up to no good, and she spoke of the *conseillers* who strolled the courtyard at lunch and the playing field in *gymnastique*, issuing commands, who were odd and strange and probably also up to no good.

Beatrice instructing me, Beatrice confiding in me, and my beginning to pierce the greyness. And the sphere frozen now, immutable, the letters no longer read.

10

February, and the crossover. Early in the morning on the day of *Carnaval*, the grey village transforming itself, unveiling itself. The old, wild demons that we had not even known were there, that lay unseen in the green hills and in the damp oak forest, rising up and taking claim of the people, and the air, and the valley itself.

There was a platform set up at the old *fronton*, the old stone handball court that lay in the forest of the Citadel, on the far side of the village. The platform, and the rectangular rim of the *fronton* were strung with streamers of red and green. The cold stone bleachers were alive with the sound of the Basque language, as colorful as the streamers that rimmed the platform and the *fronton*. It was a sunlit morning. The dark blue *gabardines* and the black umbrellas, one of which was owned by every inhabitant of this valley, lay neatly amongst the mass of people that filled the stone bleachers.

The ceremony's first sound was of the *txistu*, the Basque flute, whose music seemed to emerge out of the depths of the forest, pure, crystalline, one with the dew that filled the morning air. It began slowly, each note sounding on its own out into the morning, then gradually it gained in speed, taking on a decipherable rhythm. The rhythm intensified to a point where the notes of the *txistu* blended together in a flurry of sound. Then utter quiet, and then the slow, pure notes that emerged alone again, sounding out across the green hills.

With the second song of the *txistu* came the joining of the drumbeat, low and steady, like the heartbeat of the forest. Then began the procession of dancers, all male, all tall and strong and with the dark hair as thick as a horse's mane, wearing white pants and white shirts, red-sashed at the waist, brown leather *espadrilles* laced crisscross up the side of the lower leg, all wearing the red beret that was ceremonial, worn by no others. They came up from the far back side of the platform, one by one, stepping to the sound of the *txistu* and the lone drum whose beat was steady and even, each carrying in his right hand the dark wooden stick for which this first dance, the *Makil Danza*, was named. To the sound of the instruments they proceeded onto the platform and on to the center, forming a line from which only one emerged, stepping forward to a place of prominence in front of the line of dancers. The sound of the *txistu* and of the lone drum ceased, and the dancers stood motionless, as still as the morning air, the white and the bright red of their costumes as pure as new paint against the green of the valley and the grey of the Citadel which rose above it.

Then recommenced the *txistu*, joined seconds later by the beat of the drum. The line of dancers remaining motionless, only the one who stood in front began to move, raising the dark wooden stick high above his head. His feet went into motion, a slow step at first, then picking up speed, then into a pattern that was quicker than the eye could see. Out of the flurry of steps he leapt straight upwards, his toes pointed down. Then landing, he broke into a series of kicks, single-leg kicks and then a succession of scissor-kicks, strong and razor-sharp, reaching high above his head, the *txistu* at a crescendo.

Then suddenly the dance of the lone front dancer ceased as he brought his stick down to his side and his feet together and stood motionless, in the place that was his alone. The music of the *txistu* and of the drum stopped only for a second, and then started up again slowly, the lone front dancer remaining still, the line of dancers in back of him coming into motion. Step by step they mirrored the dance of the one, in unison, the raising up of the sticks, the initial, slow, careful movement of the feet, the increasing speed, the flurrylike pattern of the feet, the leap upward, the single-leg kicks and then the scissor-kicks, executed perfectly, but on a scale which paled against the exalted dance of the initial lone dancer. The figure in front stood motionless, face forward, while behind him, with a sameness that reflected a deliberateness, the line of dancers moved their feet in a pattern less quick, leapt to a lesser height, kicked to eye level alone.

Again the sound of the instruments ceased as the line of dancers brought down the dark wooden sticks and stood motionless behind the lone, still front figure. Then with a new burst of sound, the dancers sprang into motion, the lone front figure fading back into the line at the same instant that the line itself dissolved and reformed, breaking into a series of new patterns, sideways, endways, crisscrossed, the dancers running, leaping, the dark wooden sticks clashing high overhead with a cracking sound that joined in with the *txistu* and the drum. There was no way to tell now which dancer was he who had danced alone. Each of them, tall and strong and thick-maned, appeared to have been the one.

With the subsequent dances came the performance of the females, delicate-faced, raven-haired, gold-earringed, in red skirts, black bodices laced crisscross up the front, scarved in the ceremonial red, brown leather *espadrilles* laced up the lower leg. They came to a new music, the sweet, full sound of the accordion that rolled out wavelike through the morning. They bore baskets, and then hoops braided in red and green, and they danced in circle formation, their feet moving quickly and artfully, but in a far more gentle way than the male dancers who had preceded them. Their dance had no leaps upward, no high kicks, no scissor-kicks, and one soon recognized that the delicate pattern of the feet was repeating itself, over and over again. The dance of the females blended in with the green hills of the valley and the pale blue of the Basque sky. Theirs was the soft backdrop to the dance of the males.

And then, and then, came the dance of the *Mascarades*, that which was at once as light and wondrous as child's play, and yet more serious, infinitely more serious, than any part of the morning had been.

The dancers appeared to the lone music of the *txistu*, the pure notes sounding alone again out across the *fronton* and through the valley. First arrived the *Ensenaria*, in black pants and tunic ribbed in white braid, bearing a golden standard, stepping haltingly to the music of the *txistu*. Then came the *Marika*, red-skirted, white-aproned, in royal blue jacket ribbed in silver and gold, a flat-brimmed straw hat atop its head. Third came the *Gatuzain*, in yellow pants and scarlet tunic, moving sideways in *pas de chat*. Then the *Cherrero*, in black velvet pants and tunic, wielding a horsehair tail on a stick, sweeping the ground before him. And last, crossing the ground swept clean for him, the *Zamalzain*, the unmistakable horse figure, his beauty unmatched, in tall flowered headdress, in scarlet tunic, around his waist an oblong frame covered in scarlet cloth, the scarlet frame draped in starched white lace which hung down around his knees, the *Zamalzain* holding in front of him, at waist level, the tiny silver reins of a small horse's head which protruded from the front of the frame.

It was only when the figures were all present, in line

formation across the platform, the *Zamalzain* in the center, the *txistu* silent, that the small glass, half full of red wine, was even noticeable. It had been placed on the floor of the platform, three feet in front of the line of figures, directly before the *Zamalzain*.

To the sudden flurry of the *txistu* all of the figures but the *Zamalzain* sprang into motion, running crisscross across the platform, each in turn leaping over the half-full glass, performing turns and entrechats in the air above it. The *Zamalzain*, in all of his beauty, stood motionless, head erect, staring forward across the space through which the figures leapt.

With the slowing notes of the *txistu*, the figures returned to their places flanking the *Zamalzain*. The *txistu* silent once more, the entire line of figures stood motionless. Then once again came the notes of the *txistu*, slow and deliberate, pure and crystalline, as the *Zamalzain*, step by pointed step, emerged from the line, approaching the half-full wine glass until he stood directly before it, the glass invisible to him below the white lace which flowed from the frame about his waist. Staring forward, he leapt upwards to the new flurry of the *txistu*, toes pointed downward, redescending to the precise spot from which he had leapt. Then upwards again, his feet performing miracles in the air over the wine glass which he could not see, and down again. Then a high kick over the wine glass, then a scissor-kick, razor sharp, high over the head, recognizable to all.

And then the unbelievable feat, the notes of the *txistu* silent, the air of the late morning lying as still across the valley as the line of figures atop the platform, the *Zamalzain* leaping onto the glass which he could not see beneath the white lace cloth, raising one foot and tracing the sign of the cross in the air above the glass, then springing up, and away from the glass, the red wine unspilled. From the tension that froze the *fronton*, and the sounds of exhalation, exaltation that filled it as the *Zamalzain* leapt free of the wine glass, we knew that it was not really a dance, we knew that it was far more than a dance, this last one.

II

There was a frenzy that overtook the village as the crowd poured out of the old *fronton* and onto the road back down through the forest of the Citadel. The crowd moved quickly down toward the village, the enchanted sound of the old Basque words filling the air. Within minutes the central square was packed full. The old men in black berets were huddled together in far corners, drinking red wine and smoking hand-rolled *tabac*. Old women in black chased after small children, and young fathers and mothers filled the tables that had been set out in front of the cafés. The music of an accordion filled the square and wound its way through the cobblestone streets of the inner village, mixing with the smells of *steak-frites* and fish and fresh bread that streamed from the old dark open doorways that lined the streets of the inner core.

We the *lycéens* ran in packs that afternoon, all male or all female, crisscross through the central square, through the web of cobblestone streets, in and out of the oak forest of the Citadel. There was something in us that had not been there in the chill, disciplined class days at the Citadel, a thing that I had sensed only once before and only vaguely, all mixed up with the image of my *combinaison* and the sacred host and the ringing of the bells and the acrid smell of the *vestibule*.

But on this day of *Carnaval* there was nothing vague about it. It ignited the packs as we ran through the valley. It gathered itself into a silent, palpable zone of force each time that, in the deep of the oak forest or in one of the empty cobblestone streets of the inner village, a female pack and a male pack would cross paths, seeing each other at a distance and turning silent, each slowing its pace to a walk, approaching, until each stood motionless, fifteen feet from the other. Then in an instant the packs would spring back into motion, moving to opposite sides of the road through the forest, moving to opposite sides of the cobblestone street, circling each other, moving on at the frenzied run.

The sweet, drenched scent of the valley, it infused us on that day, and in the late night hours we lay in our beds with the red wooden shutters and the heavy windows opened up wide. The damp air of the valley flooded our rooms and ran through us, mixing with the blood of these green hills and with the name of the house and with the old, distant, familiar rhythm of the typewriter that wound on deep into the late hours.

12

The slow warming into spring, and our father's book two-thirds done by now, and we came to know the *souterrains* of the Citadel. The old, dark, earthen tunnels that wound their way silently through the underneath, that which our father never knew was there.

In the grass-covered moat, the soccer ball flying, and the girl Beatrice, raven-haired, gold-earringed, flushed with the heat of the game. She had spoken to me about the cigarettes at one of the lunch hours when it had been raining and we had taken cover in one of the sheltered areas off of the courtyard, sitting cross-legged in our *tabliers*, playing the game of bones that she carried with her. In the midst of the game she had asked out of nowhere, "Tu sais fumer?" I responded in the negative, and the look of concern had come over her face. She said that she would get hold of some cigarettes, and would show me.

And then in *gymnastique* two weeks later, in the moat amidst the spring drizzle that came every day now in late afternoon, and the soccer ball flying, the *conseillers* yelling out their commands. Beatrice was hanging way in the back, and at the point where our own *équipe* scored a goal and the moat was full of the sound of cheering, she eased over to where I stood. She said quietly that she had succeeded in buying a pack of cigarettes from the *tabac* in the village square, that she had them in her pocket. We could disappear now without anyone noticing. She looked down toward the goal at the far end of the playing field, and saw that none of the *conseillers* were looking in our direction. With a look of determination she pulled on my arm, and the two of us disappeared around the bend in the moat.

We walked the moat a quarter of the way around the Citadel, along the great stone wall that lined it, forty feet high and covered with moss and vines and dew. We stopped just under one of the old bridges that crossed over the moat, sheltered from the drizzle. Beatrice pulled from the pocket of her shorts a square blue packet that said *Gitanes* and ripped it open at the top. She pulled one cigarette out and then passed to me the little packet that was square and firm and soft at once. She pulled from the pocket of her shorts a small box of matches, and took a match from the box and struck it, and held the match to her cigarette and then to mine. The dark smoke of the cigarettes swirled around us, and then spread and dissipated in the drizzle that continued to fall.

We were on our second cigarettes when we heard the sound of voices from beyond the nearest bend in the moat. Beatrice grabbed the cigarette out of my mouth and threw both cigarettes onto the ground and stepped on them. She took hold of my arm and pulled me through an opening in the great stone wall that had been invisible, covered by foliage. She led me ten feet along a tunnel that was pitch black and earthen-floored and smelled older than anything I had ever smelled. We stood there motionless, Beatrice still holding me by the arm, somewhere deep in the earth beneath the courtyard of the Citadel. I could feel the warmth of Beatrice's body there in the darkness beside me. We could hear the voices of the *conseillers* as they passed going one way, and then as they passed back again.

We waited five minutes after the voices had passed the second time, and then Beatrice pulled me by the arm, and we proceeded through the dark toward the opening, reemerging into the green moat and the drizzle. She proceeded at a trot, with me following, up the outside embankment of the moat, across the old bridge under which we had stood, around the back side of the buildings that lined the courtyard. We darted toward the w.c. and entered it, and stood silent amidst the stench for a full minute. We darted back out, heading for the main bridge over which the class had crossed at the beginning of the hour, and crossed it, descending at a run back down the far side of the moat, onto the field where the soccer ball was flying and the *conseillers* were back to yelling their commands. Beatrice headed straight for the nearest *conseiller*, and from a distance I could see her poker look come on, baby-faced and round-eyed, as she pointed back up in the direction of the w.c.

13

The following week I went back to the *souterrains* on my own. It was after school one late afternoon, when the rain had stopped. Amid the flock of students that descended the road through the oak forest of the Citadel, *cartables* in hand and *espadrilles* soaked through, I slowed my pace until I hung far in the back. I slipped off the path, and climbed the mud-slick, leaf-strewn hillside back up towards the Citadel. I circled the moat and found the opening where Beatrice had led me, parted the foliage that covered it, and slipped into the tunnel. I dropped my blue *gabardine* onto the ground and sat down on it, cross-legged in the darkness.

I returned the next day, and the next, and then one day I brought my younger sister with me. There in the thick silence of the *souterrain*, in the damp, warm, earthen smell of the tunnels that wound their way deep beneath the courtyard floor, there was an oldness that was as dense as the earth, rounded, sheltered. It was an oldness altogether different from that sense of two thousand years that infused the view of the Citadel from the green, sunlit expanse of the esplanade. It was far older than two thousand years, far newer, unrelated to two thousand years or a million years. It attracted us in the way that a playground attracts a young child.

The girl Beatrice had led me to the *souterrains*, and yet we never again returned there together. I came to school one day carrying one of the packets of *Gitanes* that my older brother had bought at the bar-café named *Chez Garat* in the village square, and in the corner of the courtyard I opened the pocket of my *tablier* and proposed to Beatrice "qu'on s'échappe aux souterrains au cours de gymnastique." She took on the look of concern, the look of the little mother, and she said admonishingly that the *souterrains* were not a place to go, that we had gone there only because it had been necessary to hide. She said that there were things that went on in the *souterrains* that were no good, that it was not a place I wanted to go. But by then I was going there daily, and nothing of what Beatrice said seemed to have any truth to it.

I did not know the reason for it, but in the weeks that followed Beatrice began to pull away from me in a way that was so subtle, so gradual, that it was barely noticeable at first. Standing there in our place in the far corner of the courtyard, she would turn silent, looking off to other groups of girls. When I spoke she began to look at me blankly, curiously, as one looks at a stranger, and she ceased correcting me, instructing me, in any way. Then one day as we broke onto the courtyard from the lunchroom door, she headed off to a new place in the courtyard, with a group of girls from *cinquième* that I barely knew, chattering with them in Basque. I made my way into another group, that played jump-rope endlessly throughout the noon hour, and by early May Beatrice and I were no more than two *élèves* who happened to be seated next to one another in class. She came with new gold earrings one Monday, and I remembered that her thirteenth birthday was to be in May.

14

It was on a Friday in June that Beatrice spoke to me once more, only weeks before the end of the school year, only a month before our family was to return to America. The three of us had become part of this valley by now, entrenched in it, knowing the Citadel and the oak forest and the village as well as any of our classmates, on an equal footing in all of our classes, ribbing our parents for their accents indisputably American. So when Beatrice spoke to me, at the close of *mathématique* just before lunch on that Friday in June, it never once crossed my mind that I did not understand what she was saying.

There was a group of boys, and I never knew whether they might have been the same that had darkened the doorway of the *vestibule* on that day in autumn when I still knew so little that I could not dissociate the words *combinaison* and *communion* in my mind. They approached us on the road one day after school, as my younger sister and I headed down through the forest of the Citadel, the sleeves of our *tabliers* unbuttoned and rolled up to our elbows in the heat of the late spring. They were friendly in their faces, and they took our *cartables* and carried them for us, to the bottom of the oak forest where the road forked and the two of us took the right fork home.

They reappeared the next day, at the old drawbridge

just outside of the courtyard as we headed home, and they asked us for a game of soccer. We played with the group of them on the *esplanade*, in the late afternoon sun with the Citadel in the distance. They were young, barely older than me, and dark-haired and athletic. As they tore across the expanse of the *esplanade*, I saw for the first time the beauty of their faces, the dark eyes that gleamed against the green expanse, the radiant flush that the soccer game brought to their skin, the young beauty that was age-old and pure and unfaded. I remembered the dishwater coloring of the boys I had known in America, the freshly showered, scentless boys who would have been at that junior high school dance in October that was by now long past, and I understood what our father had meant when he had said that this year in this village was to be far richer than any first year of junior high school might be.

So when the group of them met us again on the path down from the Citadel, and extended the invitation for Saturday after school let out at noon, we were thrilled at the idea. They were to come with a horse that belonged to one of the boys' families, a horse for all of us to ride, and we would meet them in the grassy moat of the Citadel. We agreed readily, and in our minds we could not wait for Saturday to come.

What I understood Beatrice to be saying had much to do with the time of year, because the green hills and the fields of the valley were strewn with wildflowers in full bloom, casting a sweet scent through the valley. When said it, whispering the words "on va te violer," and looking downward as she cleared the top of her desk, I envisioned the moat of the Citadel and the horse that we would ride, and in my mind I pictured us being showered with violets, delicate and deep purple and hand-picked for us alone. What she said brought a new glow to the invitation for Saturday, a new excitement, infusing it with the beauty of the valley in full spring.

We had the sleeves of our *tabliers* rolled up and were packing our *cartables* when we arrived at twelve-thirty on Saturday, at the designated spot just below the bridge on the far side of the Citadel. From a distance we saw the group of boys standing under the bridge, their *cartables* and their white *tabliers* piled together on the grass at the edge of the moat, and yet we could see no horse. We walked side by side down the length of the green moat, scanning the area around them for any sign of a horse, and as we approached they turned silent, their faces turning in unison toward us. We stopped ten feet away from them, and stood there in silence, and without even glancing up I could see that the group of them had the same look, the same silent, motionless look of the group that had darkened the doorway of the *vestibule* in autumn.

When one of them spoke, it was as if the boundary that had formed in the air were broken, and we looked up toward the one who had spoken. He had not been able to get the family horse today, he said, but in any event we could find something to do. He dropped a soccer ball to the ground, and tapped it away with his foot, and another stopped it, and tapped it, and within a minute they were playing a sort of game amongst them, the ball passing back and forth, crisscross. We set down our *cartables* and stood there as they played, the quiet tapping sounding out into the moat. Then suddenly, one of them broke away from the group, and headed straight for the foliage that covered the opening to the *souterrain*, and disappeared inside. One of the others yelled out that we should explore the *souterrains*, and the group of them headed for the foliage, one by one disappearing through it. We stood there alone in the moat, and in the air was the grey sense of that which we knew but did not know.

From the inside of the *souterrain* one of the voices called out to us, the young sound of the voice ringing out into the moat, cleansing the air of all uneasiness, filling it back up with the pure, clean scent of the Basque spring. It filled us back up with the thrill of the afternoon, and we followed it, scampering toward the green foliage that hung down over the great wall.

It was then that we tasted it, that which lay deep beneath the beauty of the green hills, deep beneath the thick silence of the wine glass, deep beneath the courtyard of the Citadel that was laced with the clean, crisp white *tabliers*, that to which the nauseous smell of the classroom and the acrid smell of the *vestibule* and even the dark, timeless smell of the *souterrain* led, that which lived in the depth of the underneath, silent, seething. There in the darkness of the *souterrain* they were all over us, we could feel the damp, earthen floor onto which we were thrown, we could smell all over us the sweat of the *vestibule* that was as age-old as the *souterrain*. We could feel the grabbing, the pulling, the crushing weight, the dampness of the sweat, violent and inhuman, all of the unbelievable, swirling, chaotic force that lay unseen beneath the green hills showing itself here inside the secrecy of the *souterrain*.

But there was a strength in us that we had not even known we had, that gathered itself up there inside the darkness of the *souterrain*, that came from far away, that had to do with dust and sage and gnarled pine. It infused us, it infused our limbs as we scratched and clawed our way toward the opening of the *souterrain*, and it freed us, it freed us from them. Inch by inch we made it back to the opening, back through the opening, reemerging into the sparkling green of the moat, the warmth of the noonday sun, the sweet scent cast by the wildflowers in full bloom.

We descended at a run through the forest of the Citadel, down the path that led back to the house named *Goizean Goiz*, and came in through the back door, the rhythm of the Royal sounding out through the ground floor, the smell of leek soup simmering in the kitchen. We took the back staircase that led to the upstairs, unseen.

15

My father's new book finished by mid-July, and on the last evening the little fortress of five together on the front steps of the house named *Goizean Goiz*. The old Royal silent now, closed up in its case and lined up with the suitcases in the entryway. The huge black trunks that were Grandma's closed up and ready for shipping. We had filled them back up with all that we had not used, the Beatles magazines and the surfer shirts and the extra Crest toothpaste and the articles of feminine hygiene that I had not needed this year after all. We had packed them, too, with the *tabliers* and the *cartables* and the *cahiers d'étude* that we would never need again.

Our mother saying that it had been a good year. Saying that the three of us were the older and the wiser for it, that in terms of education it was beyond comparison to just one more year of school back home. Saying that the year had been good for our father, a year full of discovery and productivity. They spoke long into the evening of the beauty of the valley, of the change which the year had wrought in the three of us, of the way in which the year had made us closer, stronger, as a family.

But in my mind I was not looking back on the valley. I lay awake in my bed, waiting for morning. Frantic for the moment when we would be driving out of here, headed for Bayonne and Bordeaux and then Paris, for New York and Denver by TWA, and onward, back into the midst of the sun-baked Nevada summer, back into that other dimension that held the smell of the desert air even as you came off of the steps onto the runway. Frantic for the smell of the dust and sage and pine, and for the sight of Grandma aproned, and for the view of the deep blue lake and the pale blue maternal lake beyond it, below it, and for the sight of Grandpa waving from the quiet of the camp, his snow-white hair blowing. Frantic to head out of this valley into that separate dimension where we would next hear the sound of the Royal, where all things were new and all people freshly showered, where the buildings were new and gleaming, where the schools were new and the names were new, and the language, the language new, and clean, and lucid.

16

Beatrice. Beatrice young. Beatrice raven-haired. Beatrice gold-earringed. Beatrice maternal. She had the blood of the green hills in her. She showed me the underneath. She placed me there. I was entrusted to her. I carried the secret safely from the valley. I carried the green valley safely from the valley. Sealed. I have not touched it in twenty-five years. I have not thought of her in twenty-five years.

Beatrice poker-faced. If only you had spelled the word. If only your face had told what it meant. I did not know what you knew. I could not see what you saw. *Je n'ai pas compris. Je n'ai pas du tout compris.* I was entrusted to you.

The Entrustment

I

Grandma's dining room was packed with people on the day of our arrival, and the three of us stood there mute, still in our travel clothes, amidst the greyness that had never before been a part of this room.

Grandma was in her chair in the corner by the window, and she was wearing a dress of a kind she had never worn before, new, pastel-colored, lavender. From the double doors that led into the dining room I could see her, I could see the look on her face, wide-eyed, unfazed. I could see her smiling politely, nodding and speaking her accented "How are you?" to the people who approached her.

Family everywhere, and yet nowhere, because they were all blended in with the people who packed the room. I could catch glimpses of them, glimpses of the deep brown eyes, glimpses of the skin tanned dark with summer. And then in a split second they would have vanished, blended into the crowd that packed the room.

And the faces. The faces that had never before been a part of this room, the pale faces of the blond-haired women, the men with crew cuts, the smiles that spanned the width of the face. The crowd of them decked out in the berets of the old country, red in color, the ceremonial red. Their chests crossed with red banners that bore in gold the lettering of the name, the name that we recognized and did not recognize.

Until finally the clearing. The afternoon waning, the grey hum of their voices subsiding, the crowd of them heading one by one to the table and taking up one of the boxes piled onto it, the boxes filled with more of the red berets, more banners. The crowd heading one by one out the double doors, down the long stretch of living room and then left to the entryway, disappearing. The white lace of the tablecloth showing itself. The dining room regaining itself, the crowd one by one heading out until there remained only the familiar faces. And the circle forming around the white lace, the steam of the fresh coffee and the smell of the thick white cream and the smoke of the cigarettes filling the air, and Grandma in the corner by the window, maternal, contented.

2

And us home. The group of cousins lined up on the couch that spread along the inner wall of the dining room, and my father in the circle around the dining room table, and the look of strength and peace and promise that filled their eyes. And the clear ring of the voices, clean, lucid.

The voices picking up where they had left off nearly one year ago. The voices transparent, one with the afternoon in mid-September nearly one year ago when the old trunks that were Grandma's had been shipped off, and the keys to our house in Reno turned over to the family that would rent for a year, and we had gathered here. When here at the circle around the dining room table they had spoken of the invitation of the party to run. When they had spoken of the big-moneyed incumbent, and was there any real chance of winning. When they had spoken of how incredible it would be to actually take it. When they had spoken of their immigrant background, and how could they have a chance in hell against money and connections that went three generations back.

The voices transparent, one with the afternoon nearly one year ago when here at the circle around the dining room table there had been silence, and then out of the silence someone had spoken, someone had spoken up out of the silence and said maybe that's it, maybe our only chance in hell is to run on what we are, run our own race, to hell with the political machine. When here at the table in the dining room they had spoken of the things of which our father had written in the deep blue book, they had spoken of the old country and of the sheep camps in the desert hills, and someone had said, by God, that's what we are, that's what we'll run on.

And we had gotten out, the five of us, heading for the green hills in the wake of the huge black trunks, the suitcases and the charcoal black Royal in hand. My father with the look of pride-mixed-with-hesitation in his eyes, that the year in the green valley had now cured him of. We had the year under us and my father's new book written, and now at the circle around Grandma's dining room table there was only the strength and peace and promise in his eyes.

And the clean, lucid ring of the voices, here in the dining room in the heat of the summer, that now spoke of the proven appeal of the immigrant family. That spoke of the numbers that were showing up in the polls. That spoke of the lack of opposition in the primary. That spoke of the issues that needed addressing, and speeches and press releases that needed writing. That spoke of how the race depended on all of us pulling together. How it was the family that was running in this race. How it was the family name that would be on that ballot.

The clean, lucid ring of the voices, and the group of us lined up there along the couch against the inner wall, and Grandma in the corner by the window, contented.

3

Autumn, the rhythm of the old Royal filling our little subdivision house in Reno. Starting up early in the morning in the hour before dawn and proceeding on until eight in the morning. Resuming frantically at the

"RECINTO DEL PARADISO"—OIL ON LINEN BY AMERICAN ARTIST BRIAN SHURE, 1997.
COURTESY KATHERINE RICH PERLOW GALLERY, NEW YORK CITY

SHE JUST PICKED UP A VIRUS TO BRING HOME TO HER FAMILY AND FRIENDS.

In many parts of the world, hepatitis A virus is rampant. When you travel to those high-risk areas (shown in red on the map below*), you can easily pick up the virus from contaminated food,

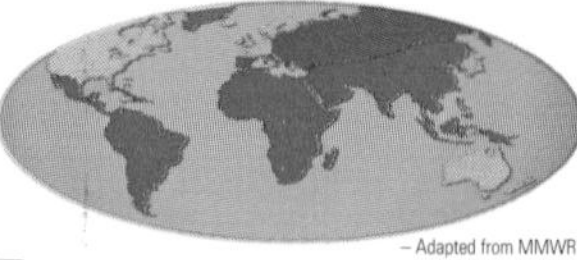

water or an infected waiter or chef... even at the best hotels and resorts. It's virtually beyond your control.

Hepatitis A can cause vomiting, abdominal pain, diarrhea, fever, nausea and jaundice (yellow skin and eyes). And you can pass hepatitis A along to your family and friends before you even know you have it.

Not only can hepatitis A make you very sick, it can also put you out of commission for a month or longer.

Hepatitis A, a highly contagious liver disease, can be easily picked up from contaminated food or water.

Up to one fifth of adults who contract hepatitis A require hospitalization... and some will die.

Why risk it? Hepatitis A can be prevented. In fact, the U.S. Centers for Disease Control and Prevention recommends immunization for travelers to intermediate- and high-risk areas. **A vaccination in advance of your trip is the best way to protect yourself against the hepatitis A virus.**

SEE YOUR DOCTOR OR HEALTH CARE PROVIDER ABOUT HEPATITIS A.

HEPATITIS FOUNDATION INTERNATIONAL

Protect yourself. Protect your family.

HA6786 1. MMWR. December 27, 1996. Vol. 45, p. 7.

*This map generalizes available data, and patterns may vary within countries.

end of the day when our father had returned from his work at the university. Our father ripping from the typewriter that which he called *copy*. Jumping into the Volkswagen squareback that had followed us home from the old country, heading straight for the highway that led to Carson.

4

A thousand people with the broad-smile faces emerging out of nowhere and circling. And the horde of us gathering, appearing before the crowd of them, greeting them, smiling and greeting them. We were a fortress, the horde of us. And the look of pride-mixed-with-wonder in my father's eyes. The look of pride in all of their eyes. Radiant. And Grandma with the look of contentment amidst the flurry, maternal.

5

We were the immigrant story.

We had the blood of the green hills in us. We bore the scent of dust and sage and gnarled pine. We were of the immigrant forebears. We had the brown eyes and the good skin. We had the hair that was in the midst of turning. We had the view from the *lookout*. We had the gleam of the deep blue lake. We had the glow of the gold-rimmed cups. We were the miraculous blend.

We wore the red berets of the old country. We crossed our chests with the red banners. The name in gold, the name spread across our chests. The old name, the name cut into the stone five hundred years old, the name of the farmhouse. The name of the boarding house. The name of those that encircled the white lace. The name that we bore. A thousand times reprinted in gold. And on buttons, and flyers, and yard signs, and billboards. Recognizable, unrecognizable. Unrestrained by a hundred generations of sameness.

6

It was early October by the time we loaded up the Volkswagen squareback that still bore the USA plaque on its back and headed down through Carson and up the highway to Spooner Summit, pulling off the highway and unlocking the gate and heading in, stopping to lock the gate up behind us. Grandpa had headed for the camp at the instant the first red beret had shown up at the U-shaped house in early June and had stayed right on through the summer, right on into the autumn that brought an early freeze to these high mountains.

We followed the road that led in, the old familiar silence descending inside the car, the cloud of dust rising up behind us. We passed the meadow lake that spread out on our right just inside the gate and took the left fork at its far end, then the gentle slope upwards. We headed into the pines that were tall and straight and thick, where the sun broke through only in threads of light, and then we broke onto the clearing, the grass expanse of meadow golden in the autumn light, crisscrossed by streambeds that were dry this time of year, awaiting the first snow. We passed the old abandoned cabin and then began the steeper climb, through the second forest of straight pines and then into the aspen, the grey-white trunks that bore the initials of sheepherders long dead, the quaking leaves that were faded green in color, awaiting the first freeze that would turn them. And then upwards, out of the aspen grove, the road riding the high ridge until it broke onto the high valley floor, rimmed on the far side by the mountains more massive, more bare, than we had ever known. We crossed the edge of the high valley floor, passing the snowflower plants that were colorless now, dry and brittle. Then upwards, into the forest of gnarled, twisted pines, the engine of the Volkswagen squareback whining with the steepness of the climb, the cold air rushing in through the open windows. And the ridge broken, and the silence broken, and the gleam of the deep blue lake below us.

And my father's voice saying that it was good to be home, and the aspen yellow gold, rimming the edge of the lake like a blaze of sunlight. The swoop downward, and the blue of the lake visible through the yellow gold of the aspen, and the swoop upwards, away from the lake. The flat, sandy area where the Volkswagen pulled off of the road, and the motor fell silent, and the doors were flung open, and we emerged, and felt the cold wind in our faces, and buttoned our jackets up tight beneath our chins. And the view from the lookout, the view from which you could see the deep blue lake below you and the pale blue expanse of Tahoe beyond it, one thousand feet below it, and above you, the clear, clear blue of the Nevada sky.

The Volkswagen squareback with the USA plaque on its back proceeding on, following the last sandy curve to the left, stopping at the last sandy ridge, the little motor barely audible as we emerged and stood and looked down into Grandpa's camp, looked down onto the white shape of the canvas tent and the shape of the old stock truck that had not moved in how many years now, and the firewood, more firewood than would be needed by the families in the space of ten years, chopped and stacked, surrounding the camp, enveloping it. And the form of Grandpa, his right arm waving, his snow-white hair blowing in the mountain air.

And the smell of the dust and pine, enveloping us, infusing us.

7

On the first Tuesday in November the U-shaped house was opened up wide. The little Indian family had been moved out of the apartment a month ago, and the entire right wing had been cleaned and opened up to be part of the house. The little table in Grandma's kitchen was filled with liquor and orange juice and soda water and ice buckets, with more unopened bottles sitting in boxes along the wall. There were clean ashtrays all over the house, and Grandma's crystal dishes, filled with nuts and olives, covered the white lace of the dining room table. A six-foot-high easel was set up in the front room of the apartment, huge sheets of white paper clipped to it at the top, each sheet labeled in black lettering with the name of a Nevada county.

By six o'clock on election night the house had a sound to it that it had never had before, a pandemonium of telephones ringing, televisions turned to high volume, the low, serious voices of our father and his brothers drifting out from the back bedrooms, drowned out by the deafening chatter of the crowd of the broad-smile people that were jammed in everywhere, all through the apartment and the old entryway, into the living room and dining room and kitchen, even into the little hallway that led to Grandma's bedroom. For short, one-minute instants the sound would cease, and the voice of a television announcer would sound alone through the house, drowned out suddenly by a wild, ecstatic cheering that shook the walls and the floor of the old house.

It was not until four in the morning that the last of the broad-smile people had headed out through the entryway, and like an old, weary body the house had seemed to sigh in anticipation of sleep. We climbed into the Volkswagen that still had the USA plaque on its back, the five of us, and headed onto the highway that led back to Reno. My father had a look of pride in his eyes that I had never seen before, as though he could not believe it, as though a God-sent miracle had struck this family of so humble roots, as though the America that they talked about in the history books had shown herself on this night, to this family.

8

Autumn moving into winter, and Grandpa still at the high-mountain camp, right through the first snow. Grandpa appearing at the U-shaped house and then two days later vanishing again, packing up his pickup and heading out to the old ranches that spotted the desert hills to the southeast.

9

Grandma dressed in lavender, her braids wrapped about her head, the delicate face that smiled politely, unfazed. The *Mother of the Year* celebration, and all of us there, the horde of us there, the fortress surrounding her, and Grandma dressed in lavender, smiling politely.

And the photograph of the delicate face, the silver-white braids wrapped about the head, there on the front page of the *Nevada State Journal*, and the caption that read *Immigrant Mother of Five*, and the print that told the story of the green hills and the sheep camps and the boarding house and the brood of five.

10

Summer, and my father handing to each of us the new book that was yellow gold in color, the color of sunlight, the color of aspen in fall.

And the words that spoke of the green valley whose beauty took your breath away. That spoke of the faces pure and radiant, unfaded, unspoiled, the old roads and the old graveyards and the old farmhouse. The mist that bathed the valley in early morning, and the colors of the oak forest in autumn. The warm, rich, sweet scent of the valley in spring. The splendor of the Citadel. The old drawbridge that his children crossed on their way to school, and the courtyard where we had played, and the grass-covered moat, the great stone wall that lined it. And the beauty of the dances, pure, and age-old. The splendor of the *Zamalzain*, hand-picked from the youth of the village, of greatest height, of strongest build, of most grace. The myth of the wine glass, the old superstition, its beauty, its charm. And the glass unspilled, the miracle feet, the miracle feat.

They were the visions that had traveled back with us, they were that which had traveled back with us together with the old familiar rhythm of the Royal, all wrapped up in the rhythm of the Royal, bound with the color of aspen in fall, entrusted to us, in the way that the deep blue book was entrusted to us.

11

My father seeing it then. Seeing it then in the way that Uncle Francis saw it then. Seeing it as clear as day, but not seeing it. The rhythm of the Royal seeing it.

12

And the voices clean and lucid, crystalline. Around the dining room table covered with white lace. And the group of us lined up on the couch along the inner wall of the dining room. And Grandma in the corner by the window, contented.

The Year of the *Alabaster*

I

Grandpa lay dying for a year and a half, in the large back bedroom, in the bed where as small children we had lain in the glow of the firelight.

He had been hit with a stroke one early morning, fully dressed, as he had come out of the door of his attic bedroom, stepping down onto the first stair. His body had turned rigid, and he had fallen like a piece of wood all the way to the bottom.

It was said to be a miracle that it had not happened when he was in the hills, or they would have found him dead. But in the privacy of our home in Reno my father would tell of how Grandpa himself had said that the stroke was not strong enough. Shaking his head, my father would say that Grandpa's eyes, as he lay in the bed, were those of a caged animal.

2

Family would come and go daily from the U-shaped house, sitting first at the chair by the side of Grandpa's bed, then heading to the kitchen for coffee and ashtray, grabbing the morning's issue of the *Nevada Appeal* from the top of the old mission dresser, settling in at the table for a half hour in the afternoon.

Over the year and a half Grandpa's skin turned paler and paler, until it was the color of the alabaster fireplace in the room where he lay. In the beginning, in his voice that was cragged from seventy years of dust and sun and wind and cold, he would ask question after question about the land, what the winter had done to the road in to the high-mountain camp, whether anyone had brought wood down for the families yet, how the road was holding out through summer. He asked whether the aspen on the rim of the lake had turned, and two weeks later for the color of the aspen on the road in, and three weeks after that for the color of the aspen in the canyon that stretched up the foothills west of Carson.

Then later he began to ask about things we never knew of, whether the gunmen at the north ranch had been dealt with, whether the lion that took out the three lambs last night had been brought down, whether the new camp tender had brought provisions from town.

And then finally he ceased talking to us altogether, lying there in the bed, as long and thin and white and strangely beautiful as the Pietà Christ, staring at us, without recognition.

Grandma would disappear from her corner by the window for a half-hour in late afternoon, and we could hear the quiet sound of their voices, the youthful, magical sound of Basque which was still a part of this house.

3

In the dining room, around the table covered with white lace, it was as if my father and his brothers too were moving from stage to stage, in their own insistent way of turning death into youth. The news of Grandpa's stroke had hit them like an arctic blast, square in the face, rolling headlong into the fanfare of the governor's annual barbeques, right into the daily glow of the newspaper headlines that were too many to clip now. They came to the dining room, all of them, and they sat silent, stunned, around the white lace, the gold-rimmed cups and the steam of the fresh coffee, filling the room with smoke.

Then one Sunday afternoon in late spring Uncle Luke came through the double doors with a new look on his face, and the old sound in his voice, that was youthful, strong, aglow with optimism, as if the stroke had never happened. He gathered them to the table, and when they were all there around the white lace, there in the dining room as Grandpa lay in the quiet of the far back bedroom, he began to speak.

He spoke of the incredible position the family was in, how the family name was the most known, the most respected, in the State of Nevada. He spoke of the race for the United States Senate, to come one year from this fall. He spoke of what a national office would do for the family name. He spoke of how the family name would take on a significance far beyond the confines of the State of Nevada. He spoke of the wide-open field of opportunity that it would create for all of us, and our children after us.

He spoke of how the race would be easier this time, how they were coming in with experience, how they would be running on an established name. He spoke of the whole brigade of loyal supporters who were silently out there, all across the state, ready to spring into action at the first sign.

He spoke, there at the circle around the white lace as Grandpa lay in the quiet of the far back bedroom, and by the time the afternoon had waned, the glow of optimism, the glow of new endeavor, had spread to all of them. It rose up, there at the dining room table, encircling it, filling the air where the cold chill of Grandpa's stroke had hung.

And the voices regained, against the quiet of the far back bedroom.

4

The voices regained, and the thrill of new endeavor, and Grandpa lying in the quiet of the far back bedroom, and Grandma in the corner by the window, with the thread of distance that was far too subtle to even put your finger on.

5

The end of her own life signaled by Grandpa's coming home to lie in the far back bedroom, Grandma turning to us, becoming one of us, the nineteen, the good-skinned nineteen. Winking secretly as we flooded in and out of the U-shaped house, the oldest of us college age now, appearing at the double doors on weekends and at school breaks in faded jeans and embroidered overalls, beaded, hair straight and ragged and sun-bleached. Grandma's body old and warm and sweet-smelling there in the corner by the window, and the silken braids wrapped about her head, and the youthful secret winking. Signaling us secretly, slipping us ten-dollar checks as we came and went.

And the distance, the thread of distance, the voices regained.

6

In summer, when one of us had come alone, spending a few minutes at Grandpa's side and then heading for the kitchen, grabbing coffee and ashtray and newspaper and settling in alone at the dining room table, Grandma would sit peacefully in her corner by the window, and then the old look of mischief would come over her face. She would wonder aloud if by any chance we felt like a strawberry milkshake, and we would bring her her purse and take the dollar bills she held out to us, and head out the double doors barefoot, following the old route through the back streets to Main Street, heading right at the corner for the Penguin Ice Cream Stand. We would return with two milkshakes in hand, and sit quietly with her, in the still of the afternoon. She sipped the milkshake slowly, looking off out the window for timeless intervals.

7

There was an afternoon when the heat had not let up, and she had gone to her room to nap, and I looked in on her, and found her seated on the side of the bed, dressed only in her slip, her heat-swollen feet soaking in a small pan of water that lay on the floor. And I bathed her, I took the washcloth that lay in a bowl of cool water on her nightstand beneath the post where the dark rosaries hung, and squeezed it, and ran it over her shoulders and down along her arms and up onto her back and onto the nape of her neck beneath the part in her hair for the pinned-up braids. And I dried her feet, and powdered her. And then as she turned and laid her old weary body down I climbed onto the bed and stretched out beside her, my young sun-darkened limbs next to her.

In the quiet of the bedroom I could hear the gentle, wavelike sound of her breathing, and I was bathed in the warm good scent of her.

8

Grandpa's funeral came on a Friday in late November. The first snow had fallen a week earlier, covering the high mountains all the way to their base, dusting the valleys and the foothills, closing off the road to the high-mountain camp until June. The sidewalk in front of Saint Theresa's Catholic Church was covered with patches of ice, and people were walking slowly, picking their steps, sticking close to the little wrought-iron fence that rimmed the churchyard. The cars filled the parking lot that lay to the east of the church, and were lined up along both sides of the street for a quarter-mile in each direction.

9

We gathered in the cold of the parking lot, the horde of us, shivering under our coats, bleary-eyed from the two days that had preceded this Friday morning, the two days that had followed the moment on Wednesday, in early afternoon, when Grandpa had lain in the far back bedroom and had simply stopped breathing, setting the family in motion like the parts of a machine.

Within an hour, the news had spread by telephone wires to every one of us, crisscross through Carson City and on out to Reno, on out to those of us off to college in Palo Alto and Denver and Portland and Phoenix. By five o'clock the suitcases had been thrown together, the cars headed out onto the highways, the planes boarded, and by eight every one of us had come through the old front door of the U-shaped house.

We had crossed through the old entryway that smelled of must, veering left through the inside door, swinging it closed behind us, heading down the long stretch of living room. We had passed the mass of photographs atop the baby grand, we had come through the open double doors into the dining room where the stove was blazing and the voices were familiar, where Grandma sat quietly in her corner by the window where the shade was drawn down, where family was everywhere, and no one was there who was not family.

Grandpa had been taken away and then returned to the far back bedroom, dressed in clean white bedclothes and laid in clean white sheets, half sitting. The fire in the alabaster fireplace had been lit, and it cast a glow on the room and on the body, on the figures in the room and on us as we were led in, one by one.

My father and his brothers were seated around the side of the bed, and they were talking in low, quiet voices. On his lap Uncle Francis held a square pad of white paper, and you could hear them guiding him, noting the strength of the jaw, the slant of the cheekbones, the snow-white hair that was still as thick as a horse's mane. As though together they were trying to capture it, tame it, the face that had come in and out of their lives since childhood, disappearing and appearing and disappearing again.

10

Thursday, sleepless, scurrying, amidst a gentle second snow, when Grandpa was taken away again, and the responsibilities for church and priest and music, for casket selection and flower selection and seating arrangement were assigned among them, when the old black telephone in Grandma's dining room rang off the hook, the buzzer in the old front entryway sounding the arrival of more and more telegrams, Grandma sitting quietly in her corner by the window amidst the scurrying, the room full of the smell of coffee brewed pot after pot, of cigarettes lit one after the next.

II

Grandma was already in the church when Uncle Luke spoke to us, there in the parking lot on Friday morning, in his voice that was strong and young, sounding out through the frozen air. He told us how grown up we all looked, the boys in slacks and jackets, the girls in dresses and stockings and sleek shoes, and he told us to put our best faces forward, our strongest faces, as a family. He directed the boys to the casket that now lay at the foot of the steps, and he lined the rest of us up on the sidewalk, by age, in back of the group that was composed of Grandpa's children.

It must have taken us ten minutes to make the entrance, because the church was more full, they said later, than it had been on any prior occasion. The people were crowded into the entryway that smelled of incense, spilling over into the halls that led to the side rooms of the church, and as we entered they pushed up against each other, making room for the casket and then for the stream of us that filed in. From the back of the church you could see the sea of people that filled the pews and the side aisles. You could see Grandma sitting alone in the front pew, to the right of the center aisle where the boys were placing the casket, and the empty pew beside her, the two rows of empty pews behind her. We filed down the center aisle slowly, one behind the next, feeling the faces of the crowd turn to us, finally reaching the empty pews and turning into them, filling them row by row. Kneeling, we performed the sign of the cross and bowed our heads downward.

In the silence before Mass was to begin, we turned our eyes to the altar, to the twin golden chalices that sat atop a white linen cloth, to the flowers that overflowed the altar, their scent permeating the air of the church. We looked over to Grandma, we looked at her lavender dress, her silver-white braids wrapped about her head. We looked at the group of her children that filled the front pew beside her, the five of them together, radiating that aura of indomitable unity, that aura of family, which had brought them here to this day when the death of their immigrant father was known by all of Nevada. We felt the strength of our own group, filling the two pews in back of them, the group bound by the eyes and the good skin and the common heritage, the common blood.

12

The crystalline notes of the *txistu* seemed to come out of nowhere, sounding out one by one, lone and pure, the old sound that was as young as the morning, the magical sound of the green valley and the oak forest. They wound their way down the aisles and through the pews and up onto the altar and back out again, bathing the church, filling the air, enchanting it.

13

Then silence, and after the silence the emergence of the priest, in white robe, gold-trimmed, proceeding out onto the altar, turning, and kneeling before the golden chalices atop the white linen cloth. Then rising, and turning, and moving forward toward the crowd, closing his gaze in on the group of us that lined the three front pews, pronouncing the first words of the old liturgy that had not been heard in this church in years, *Dominus vobiscum.* He turned back to the altar and to the chalices, the white robe flowing down around him, and kneeling and rising, he commenced the steps of the Mass, sounding out the language of the old liturgy, crisscrossing the altar, kneeling and rising each time at the center.

There was a lull at the moment the consecration was to begin, and a shuffling in the front pew, and into the center aisle emerged Uncle Luke, the eldest of them. He moved into the space beside the casket, facing the altar and kneeling, rising and proceeding forward up the steps of the altar, kneeling, then rising and turning, proceeding to the right of the altar, to the podium and the microphone which protruded from it.

He looked out on the sea of faces and spoke to them as only he could speak to them, welcoming them, thanking them on behalf of all of us for their presence on this cold morning in November.

Then from behind the podium he brought out that which he had carried in his hand, that which no one had yet noticed but which was now recognized by all, holding in front of him the book that was deep blue in color, that bore the family name on its edge, the book that told the story of their father. He opened it, and turned the pages to the place which he had marked, and looked up to the sea of faces, and commenced reading the familiar words that were pure poetry, the words that sang of the boy born to the green hills, that sang of the hope and promise that lay in the desert hills of a new land, that sang of the dashing of the hope and promise and the strange beauty of the man that emerged out of it. Our uncle read the words in a voice that was one with the language of the deep blue book, and in the end, as he folded the book closed and proceeded down from the altar, dissolving back into the group that lined the front pew, it was not certain which of the brothers had spoken to the crowd this morning, our father or our uncle, or rather, it was as if both had.

14

Then reappeared the figure of the priest, moving across the altar, to the place in the center where the chalices sat atop the white linen cloth, kneeling before them, the crowd rising and kneeling after him, like a wave. The sound of the old liturgy rose up again, echoing out through the church, building to a crescendo.

And then silence, the timeless silence that is the soul of the Mass, the faces of the crowd turned downward, the priest unseen, kneeling down before the holy table, kneeling before the chalices atop the white linen cloth, tracing the sign of the cross in the air in front of them.

Then out of the silence the voice of the priest springing up again, the crowd looking up, rising, moving out of the pews and into the aisles and forward to the altar rail.

15

The horde of us moving into the aisle, the fortress of us moving into the aisle, and blending into the crowd that filed forward, and the look in Grandma's eyes as we passed in front of her. The look of distance that cast itself over the whole church, over the crowd and over us blended in with the crowd and the priest and the flowers. The look that made no sense, that had no logical connection to anything, to the beauty of the funeral or the beauty of the family or to anything that had taken place this morning.

The Sacrifice

I

January, Carson City snow-covered, the dining room at the U-shaped house filled with the warmth of the blazing stove. The flurry of the senatorial campaign beginning to gather itself. The dining room table covered with boxes filled with the thousands of communications that had poured in on the occasion of Grandpa's death. Filled with the letters of condolence from office holders throughout the state, and the monetary contributions to scholarship funds, and the gifts of flowers, and telegrams, and the two formal gift certificates by which Grandpa was enrolled for overlapping periods of one year after death in the State of California Province of the Jesuit. Filled with the cards and letters from people who had known one of the five of them at some time recent or long past, and from people who had never known them but who had long admired them, who had read the book that told the story of their father, or had voted for Uncle Luke, and usually both. The communications amassed in cardboard boxes atop the dining room table and then carted off to an office where a card file system was set up alphabetically, listing name, address, and nature of communication or gift, checked off one by one as the letters of appreciation were typed out.

Grandma in the window corner, silent.

2

Early summer, the faces reemerging out of the woodwork, the faces which had lost in youth but which still bore the same broad smiles, resurrecting the red berets that years ago had been stored away as souvenirs. Flooding into the U-shaped house, flooding into the dining room and filling it. Carting boxes to and fro. The name stretched in gold across their chests, our name, the name that glowed.

Grandma in the window corner, silent.

3

July, the broad-smile faces filling the dining room in the heat of the Nevada summer, and for reasons of common courtesy the impossibility of closing the double doors when the need for private discussion arose.

And the retreat. The drive up the highway to Spooner

Summit, and the pulling off of the highway just in front of the gate. Opening the gate and closing it and locking it and heading in, and the silence descending inside the vehicles. Passing the meadow lake and heading upwards, into the tall, straight pines, breaking onto the clearing, passing the old abandoned cabin and heading into the thicker forest of straight pines, and then the aspen, the grey-white trunks into which the initials were carved, and the leaves green with summer. And upwards, riding the high ridge and breaking onto the high valley floor, covered by wildflowers pale in color, past the first snowflower bright red in color, and upwards, into the twisted, gnarled pines, the air pure and cold through the windows, and the breaking of the ridge, and the silence broken, and the gleam of the deep blue lake. And the swoop downwards, the blue of the lake visible through the aspen leaves green with summer, and the swoop upwards, and the stopping and getting out, and the view from the lookout, the cold wind in our faces, the deep blue lake below and the pale blue, maternal expanse of Tahoe a thousand feet below it, and the clear, clear blue of the Nevada sky. And the proceeding on, and the last sandy ridge, and the view down on the place that smelled of dust and gnarled pine. The five of them. And we went with them.

And we were young adults now. There in the camp where only family entered. There in the place still enveloped by firewood chopped and stacked. There at the campfire, beneath the old stars that gleamed as brightly as though newly born, there around the coffee and the cigarettes transported. Their actually looking to us. Their asking us for *gut reactions*. For the first time our sensing that we had something to do with it, the name.

4

The dining room filled with the broad-smile faces, and filled with the heat of early August, and the promise of victory, radiant, and Grandma.

5

Late August, a Wednesday, and the look in my father's eyes as he came through the front door of our house in Reno. The afternoon of the debate telecast live to the entire state, and the opponent, and the uttering of the allegation that was black in color, as brutal and deadly as if the opponent had pulled a revolver and aimed and shot across the room filled with microphones and cameras. My father coming through the front door of our house in Reno with murder in his eyes.

6

Followed by Saturday afternoon, the old heavy front door of Grandma's house closing, and the door into the living room closing, and the old double doors closing. And at the dining room table covered with white lace the five of them forming that circle which we knew had existed but which we had never seen, the circle that had begun as a place of protection and had become a place of privilege and which was now, again, a place of protection. The five of them stone silent around the white-laced table, and the group of us lined up on the couch against the inner wall, and Grandma in the corner by the window, silent.

Then our Uncle Luke speaking up, in a voice that we

had never heard before, a voice that had lost its warm ring of optimism but which was trying for it, insisting on it, in the way that the children of immigrants had once pulled themselves up by their bootstraps in the privacy of this very room. Saying that it was a fact that we were going to have to live with, that any family that tried to do something good in this world was at some point going to come up against those that will try to turn all good things into bad. Asking how the hell they had come this far if they did not have the stuff of which fighters are made. Saying that they would counter it pure and simple, and put the opponent in his place.

But then Uncle Francis speaking up, in his voice that was rational, incisive, crystal clear. Saying that which the rest of them knew but did not want to hear, saying that no matter how you looked at it, the fact remained that the family name had been tarnished. Saying that with little more than two months remaining before election day, in no sense could a simple refutation be counted on. Saying that it was going to have to be something greater than that, something major, something that would restore the name in the eyes of the voters.

The group of us lined up on the couch against the inner wall of the dining room, and Grandma in the corner by the window, silent.

7

We have no memory of who first said it, but suddenly it was there, amidst the steam of the coffee and the smoke of the cigarettes, the image of the deep blue book, the book that was the first to flow out of the lovely rhythm of the old Royal, the book for which we had been given champagne as small children, the book that you could hold under one arm as you escaped from a fire, the book that was part of what we were. Suddenly they were talking about it, about the story of our grandfather, about the story that told of their heritage, that showed where they came from and what they were made of. They were talking about paperback printing, and the speed at which mass production could be done, and how a simple yellow band could be printed across the upper right corner of the cover, reading *Special Election Edition*. They were talking of the genius of the idea, the brilliance of it, and with each sentence the voices were regaining their ring, the crystalline ring that went with the top of the table.

8

The voices crystalline, and Grandma in the corner by the window, and the look in my father's eyes as he walked out of the U-shaped house that day, the look of confusion so deep that it swirled.

9

And the broken, rhythmless sound of the typewriter that began the next morning, stammering, invading the little subdivision house in Reno, filling it.

10

Late autumn, the aspen that rimmed the canyon in the foothills turned radiant by now, and the radiance of the victory that was a victory by four hundred votes.

11

And in the aftermath, that which was unseen beneath the radiance of the victory. The stammering of the Royal. And the voices crystalline. And the circle around the white lace radiant. We were the miraculous blend.

12

There was a day in early January, after Uncle Luke's departure for Washington, D.C., when the sun had come out and there was a hint of warmth to the air. The streets were wet with melting snow, and in the Volkswagen squareback that was mine now, rusting on its bottom rim, I had driven up to the U-shaped house in early afternoon.

I came in the old front door and veered left, through the musty smell of the entryway and into the long stretch of living room, and found the dining room empty of people, more quiet than I had ever known it to be. I headed for the kitchen and started a fresh pot of coffee, grabbed an ashtray and the *Nevada Appeal*, and settled in at the dining room table. I figured Grandma had gone to her room to nap.

It was an hour later when I rapped lightly on the door to Grandma's little bedroom, and opened it, and found the bed untouched, the old dark rosaries hanging down over the bedpost. I went down the little hallway, into the back bedroom where the alabaster fireplace had not been lit since the night of Grandpa's death, and found the little door that led outside opened. I headed out through the screen door, onto the concrete porch where the kittens used to come for milk, the small place that trapped the afternoon sun. And found her there, sitting in a chair in the shade of the eaves, dressed in the black wool dress that had not been worn in years, the black wool scarf that had not been worn in years covering the pinned-up braids, draping her shoulders.

She did not even look at me. She was as lucid as any of us that were full of youth and full of vigor, and yet she was farther away, farther away from all of us, than she had ever been before. I knew she had gone back to the green hills.

PART TWO

The Good Skin

I

Your body, your body that was old and good, it has been the thread. By which we have made our way through the labyrinth of the twenty years that were to come, that have come. The thread by which we have found our way out from the dark tunnels of the underneath. By which we have found our way to that which all along you knew. You knew.

Because it was done then, wasn't it, Grandma, the day the deep blue book was given up, although we did not know it, we could not see it. We who knew things that went light years beyond that which you had any hope of knowing. We could not see beneath the white lace. We could not see what you knew even then.

Twenty years of their denying it, of our denying it in our own separate way. We are so different from them, and yet so much the same.

All by that golden thing, that which we now know was it, that which gleamed at the center of the table, that which hovered there at the spot where the cream and sugar sat. That which rose up amidst the steam and the smoke to claim the deep blue book, that which having claimed the deep blue book would move on, devouring more, until it devoured the very thing for which it itself stood, insatiable.

And you knew it then, you knew that we could not see what was there before our eyes, that which showed itself as plain as day in the rhythm of the Royal, the rhythm that like the old language had been the music by which we lived, the broken rhythm that was as clear a message as we could have asked for.

And you saw them leaping, and us leaping in our own separate way, leaping above that which we could not see, leaping from the last leap, then leaping from that last leap, and on and on. Until the day when having searched out the underneath we would find it, we would see it.

And would clutch to the warm scent of your good body to make our way out of it.

2

The baby boy, my baby boy, he was for you, Grandma, although you never saw him, held him, knew him. Because I know now that he was conceived on that afternoon five years before his own birth, on that afternoon when the deep blue book was there in the dining room amidst the steam of the coffee and the smoke of the cigarettes. I know now that he was conceived for a purpose, in the way that the five of yours marked your own presence in the new world.

But this one's purpose was altogether different. He was like the deep blue book. He was to be the deep blue book. He would come dark-eyed and good-skinned, bearing the beauty of the green hills. He would bear the scent of dust and sage and promise and gnarled pine. He would be the untarnished link. He was for your eyes. Through him you would see what we were.

3

To think back on what he was born out of. The radiance. The radiant glow that encircled us and the voices crystalline and the stammering and you retreated and the insistence on the radiance.

And entrustment, the idea of it, he was born out of that too. My packing up the Volkswagen squareback that was rusting on its bottom rim, and boxing up and storing away the literature books and the papers, the stack of papers by which I had thought I would be a writer someday, and amidst the stammering heading for law school. Driving out in the heat of late summer, heading out across the state with which the family name was synonymous by now, the state where even in partial absence the family was as present as the dust and sage and pine. Eastward, crossing the western states and then heading into the midwestern states, two thousand miles away from you who had retreated. And there finding a place amidst the rows of freshly showered students. Khakied. Thinking I had the blood of lawyers in me. And here amidst the English language that was new and clean and lucid finding it, here in the midst of the rows of students the old greyness that I recognized and did not recognize, the grey words that were new and thick and palpable and had no meaning.

Here too. And then the early morning on the first day of the second semester of Law I. And the ring of the professor's voice. And the word that emerged out of the greyness, the pure word, the golden word, the word that had the magical, musical sound of the old language that was part of the U-shaped house. *Fiduciary*. The professor uttering it, and the clear ring of it through the classroom, and the lifting of the greyness, the piercing of it.

And the idea of entrustment. The magical word encircling the idea of entrustment, flowing out from it. The image of entrustment, the image of a thing of value, and the handing of it, the entrusting of it, to another. And flowing from that act the recognition of control, by which he who holds the valuable thing obtains power, assumes power, over it. And flowing from that control the recognition of strength, residing in him who holds control, and from there the recognition of weakness, of vulnerability, residing in him who has entrusted the valuable thing. And flowing from the strength of the one and the vulnerability of the other the recognition of duty, duty of a special nature, of an exalted nature, running from him who holds control to him who is powerless, to preserve and protect the valuable thing. And flowing from the duty the recognition of that on which the duty was founded, on which the entrustment itself was founded, called faith. And from it the word for the duty, the word that had sprung out of the greyness, *fiduciary*.

And the understanding of it, the knowledge that the new word that was clean and lucid and radiant was as old as the blood that ran in me. The recognition of it, the recognition of it from the instant of its first uttering, the image of the table springing up there in the classroom in early morning, the image of the table covered with white lace and the five of them encircling it and the group of us beneath it and the dark limbs of entrustment that ran crisscross through the underneath, connecting them, connecting us to them. And that which glowed, that which glowed there at the center atop the white lace at the place where the cream and sugar sat, the recognition of it, the understanding of it. The intersecting point, it was the intersecting point.

4

The sphere of remembrance taking form there inside the ring of the golden word, there in the deep inside of me and carried with me into the rows of freshly showered students in early morning, untouched.

And nourished, nourished there in the evening hours in the privacy of a student apartment, nourished by that which came over the airwaves that spanned the country from Washington, D.C., the uttering of the name, your name, our name. And together with it the phrases that were as tied to it as the dust and sage and pine, *family from Nevada*, and *immigrant mother*, and *immigrant father*. Nourishing the sphere, the sphere that looked back on the state and envisioned the places which smelled of dust and sage and pine, and aspen the color of sunlight, and the gleam of the deep blue lake, and the lovely rhythm of the Royal, and you aproned, standing to pour fresh coffee to those that encircled the white lace.

5

And the finding of the father.

And the breathing of life into the sphere.

And then the first sign of physical form, the nausea there in the pit of my stomach, there in the midst of the rows of freshly showered students in early morning. And then the first small weight of it.

The infant who just in time had begun to grow in me, I thought, just in time because it was in the midst of that year when your old legs had finally given out, and the first of the little strokes had already come, and we knew that it was not far off now, you did not have much time to last. The infant form who from his first moment was in a race against your death. To be shown to you. To be anointed by you. To be held against your body that was old and good and to be anointed by you.

6

Shielded. There in the church where we had sat next to you, there in the pews where we had sat next to you, the huge roundness that was my abdomen held closely, shielded. The acrid scent that hung in the pews of the family section. Your body as cold as stone in the aisle. The infant that had lost the race against your death. Still of rounded form, shielded.

It was the same, Grandma, it was the same, here in the church where we had sat with you, the smell that we had long forgotten, the smell that was in the tunnels of the green valley that we had thought we had left behind, the smell that was in the things that we had not thought of in years, the smell of the objects of the *Citadel* that had arrived in your own huge black trunks and then were stored away, sealed, the smell sealed in but *here*, here in the place that existed in a separate dimension from the green valley and now somehow let loose, somehow let loose in the pews of the family section not three feet from your body, as here in the church as the crystalline notes of the *txistu* had been on the occasion of Grandpa's death.

And to think that we were *shielding* ourselves from it. To look back and to see that from what we know now, to look at the sunbathing on the first beach day at Lake Tahoe, and to think that there in the church on the day when your body lay as cold as stone in the aisle we were shielding ourselves from it. And to think that I had my arms wrapped about the rounded sphere, shielding it.

7

And to think back on the events by which it was let loose.

To think back on how it could have been kept sealed in, if only we had seen it, if only we had known it was there.

And to think that it was accomplished by then, to think that even then there would have been nothing we could have done about it.

To think back on how your not taking the next breath

had set the family in motion like the parts of a machine. To think back on how the news had struck out from Carson, as on the occasion of Grandpa's death, lighting up the telephone network but more expansive this time, spanning the country from Carson City to Washington, D.C., and then from those points on out crisscross, to colleges and apartments bordering on graduate schools and law schools in Phoenix and Palo Alto and Iowa City and Spokane. And the bags thrown together, and the planes boarded by two in the afternoon. And the flooding in, the flooding into the state to stand for the last time next to your body that was old and good.

But then the gathering, Grandma, the gathering at the house that was new and foreign, the house that was not yours or ours or anyone's who was family. That was made of tinted glass and new wood, that sat on a hill overlooking the night lights of Reno, that belonged to a lawyer whom we knew and did not know, whom Uncle Luke knew.

And the five of them on the balcony in late evening, and we knew that they were talking about the land, the lower land that stretched up the foothills west of Carson, that held the peninsula and the blaze of aspen. They were talking out there on the balcony, and we barely noticed them until there was a break in the talk. Then there were voices again, and then a longer break, then voices that were a notch lower, and then we didn't hear any voices. And the sliding door flying open, and through it came the figure of my father, and in his eyes there was no confusion this time, but anger, anger of a kind we had never seen before.

The machine gone haywire, Grandma, not ten hours after your death.

8

My mother spreading a white lace tablecloth over the table of our subdivision house in Reno, and the gathering of us, into the late hours of the night of your death. And the old familiar sense of the small fortress, and the new, strange sense of it. And the thing that turned the color of my father's eyes from brown to black. And my arms wrapped about the rounded sphere. And we were adults now, we were part of it. And the limbs that ran unseen through the darkness of the underneath.

And the image of the land rising up there at the table. The image of the canyon that stretched up the foothills west of Carson. And the image of the aspen that rimmed it, bright yellow gold, the color of sunlight. And the smell in summer. And the smell in winter. And Grandpa stooping. And Grandpa bounding, disappearing. And Grandpa in his deathbed in the far back bedroom. And his skin the color of the alabaster. And Grandpa asking for the color of the aspen.

And the dark thing, the thing that changed the color of the eyes. And the sentence from which it had flowed, the simple sentence, the clear, lucid sentence that the land should be sold. And the remembrance of the deep blue book that had told the story of our grandfather. And the image of Grandpa stooping, and bounding. And the stammering of the Royal that had not let up beneath the radiant glow. And the dark thing that now came out of the issue of the land.

9

And the gathering in the early morning next to your body, and the acrid smell that hung in the pews of the family section, and the crowd that had no inkling of it. And the eyes of those who had formed a separate table, the rage of a kind we had never had the sight of before, the rage that flowed from the unimaginable break in the old indomitable circle, that changed the color of the eyes from brown to black. And the crowd having no inkling of it.

And the rounded sphere not ten feet from your body and shielded. And out of the shielding the rescue of it. The knowledge that he could not be brought into the world there. Not there where the U-shaped house sat empty, not there amidst the broken sound of the Royal, not there where the dust and sage and pine had lost its scent. Not there in the place which housed the objects of the *Citadel*, the smell let loose. Good God, how for so many years we could have forgotten that smell.

The rescue in the face of all odds, because the doctors said one week, two at the outside, no chance to last out the plane trip. And my boarding the plane, fastening the seat belt below the rounded form, and lasting out the ride. And delivering him, there in the place that was two thousand miles from that which he was.

Safe, dark-eyed, good-skinned, untouched and untarnished, amidst the remembrance of the dust and sage and gnarled pine, and aspen the color of sunlight, the gleam of the deep blue lake, and the music of the old language, and the lovely rhythm of the Royal, and you aproned.

Entrusted.

10

The name. Your name, their name, our name, it was still out there, and it was untouched.

And the child, my child, your child, I shielded him from that too. There in the apartment that bordered on the midwestern campus, there in the apartment where I sat cross-legged before the evening news, there where with his father the dark-eyed child lay dozing, it would invade on the airwaves from Washington, D.C., right into the calm of the apartment, sudden, unexpected. And I would jump, fly across the room and squelch it, silence it, before the phrases that were attached to it had even had the time to be uttered.

And then I would take the child, take him and hold him there in the apartment where the television screen was now black, and sing to him the songs that my father had sung to us as small children, the songs that were tied to the old rhythm, tied to the taste of champagne in midafternoon. And sniff him, sniff the smell of his limbs that was clean and good, untouched.

Because even then, even then in the aftermath of your funeral when the crowd had had no inkling of that which was there in the pews of the family section, even as early as that the name had lit out, detached from us, gleaming, jewellike, untouched. It had struck out untouched and it had been to a million places we did not know. And it had a new ring to it, Grandma, even then it had the hint of a smile to it. Even then it had become a separate thing, it was not your name, it was not our name, it was not anyone's name.

II

The baptism.

Two years later and we came back. Packing up the Volkswagen and packing up the law books, and packing the two-year-old in safe, and heading back. To the place, to *this* place, to which he was as tied as the dust and sage and pine.

There had been a buffer of time. Time for the issue of the land to be resolved, the bottomland parceled, the high-mountain land found to be indivisible, but nonetheless divisible through a mechanism of the law called time shares. Time for the U-shaped house to be sold and look lived in again. Time for the smell to subside, time for the state to regain its scent. Time for the old rhythm to return to my father's house, plenty of time. And for the dark thing to fade from the eyes, plenty of time for the old color to return, gentle brown.

The buffer of time, and the old Volkswagen heading back into the state, and the sweet scent through the open windows, the two-year-old breathing in his own scent borne on the wings of the desert air, and the shielding. The old Royal stone cold, the old rhythm no longer even a part of the house, no longer even what you thought you heard for that brief instant in early morning as you crossed out of sleep.

And the eyes, good God, the eyes that had come out of the buffer of time, the eyes that went with the cold silence of the rhythm, the eyes identical to the eyes of the child. What is it, Grandma, what is it about eyes that are identical, and yet as different as night and day? Shielding him, shielding the child from that which the buffer of time had wrought. The dark thing gone, but no gentle brown, no gentle brown and no rhythm either, the child's gentle brown eyes looking at the identical eyes where lay emptiness as deep as the earth.

And the rescue, the child tucked under one arm, heading from the car down the dusty path through the rows of headstones. And the quiet hour, there beneath the blue of the sky, the incredible blue of the sky, there amidst the scent of the desert air, the child at play in the dust, covered with the dust, bathed in it, anointed.

12

The purpose sparked on the afternoon seven years past now. The purpose of replacing the deep blue book, the purpose of being it. The purpose of denying the afternoon its existence, the purpose of curing us of it. The purpose that was dark-eyed and good-skinned, anointed.

13

Out of the underside of the name the invitation came.

Early summer, and the call from the cousin who we had always said was the most like you. Who years ago had headed for Washington with her father. And had come back to the state for a summer visit. And telephoned, and asked, why not get together with her father and her for lunch. And my stuttering and groping, and saying that I would call her back. My telephoning my father's house and telling my mother to put my father on, and my reiterating the invitation. Then the silence that lasted for two minutes, and then the voice that was out of the past, strong, full, unhesitating, "You go to the lunch."

There at the table in the crowded restaurant, there at the table with my cousin and her child and mine, I could not cease envisioning the morning when we had stood next to you, Grandma, the morning that would always be as long past as the child was old, three years now, almost to the day. And the sense of the small fortress, and the thing that changed the eyes from brown to black. But then out of it Uncle Luke appeared, and it was a magical thing, his face as warm and glowing as in the old days of the U-shaped house.

And the easy talk, there at the table in the crowded restaurant, clean, lucid. How adult we were all getting to look. How busy life was in Washington. Magical, as if nothing had happened, except that there was no mention of my father.

And me comfortable at the table, and clear-minded as a bell, until the point when I happened to glance at his hands, which were placed on the rim of the table as the order for coffee was taken. And then suddenly, the whole room starting to come unraveled, me staring down at the hands and seeing my father's hands, identical, indistinguishable. My looking up, and the eyes of Uncle Luke riveted on the face of my three-year-old, on the child's eyes that were identical to the eyes of my father. And in the split instant before his eyes darted away, my seeing my father's eyes there too, there in the eyes of Uncle Luke that for that second were indistinguishable, the eyes that had gone through the identical phases of strength, and peace, and confusion, and black anger, and emptiness as deep as the earth.

And there in the midst of the crowded dining room, the word *fiduciary* springing up, the golden word, the word that by now I had studied and analyzed and understood inside and out, the word that suddenly I realized I had never understood at all. Because there in my uncle's hands and in his eyes was the whole other side of fiduciary duty, the side of which the law did not speak, the whole other side under which there is a duty owed to the creature called family, under which the creature is entrusted to each of its members, under which the *stronger* the family, the more valuable it is, the more *vulnerable* it is, the more needful of protection.

And the image of the old table springing up there in the crowded restaurant, the table that was made of dark wood and was lace-covered. And the knowledge, the knowledge, that that which lay at the center of the table atop the white lace, that which glowed, that which gave the crystalline ring to the voices that surrounded the underneath, was more than an intersecting point. It was its own thing. It was that separate thing called family. And it alone was the valuable thing. To it all limbs led, to it all gifts were owed. It had always been that way. For ten thousand years it had been that way.

14

The purpose. He was it, wasn't he, Grandma, there at the table in the crowded restaurant, seated there, pure and untouched, dark-limbed with early summer, taking us back, taking us back and cleansing us of the afternoon, curing us of it? Curing us of the afternoon and of the confusion that filled the eyes and the halting rhythm, curing us of the dark thing that changed the color of the eyes, curing us of the silence, the hollow silence of the Royal and the eyes that went with it. By which we would spring from the silence, leaping.

Dear Uncle Luke, I began the letter. I wrote of the chasm that had hung over the table in the crowded restaurant. And of how devoted my father had been to him. How when one really thought about it, the dissenter is the one whose devotion is certain to have all along been most true. How if only the family could be put back together. How if only the family could be put back together.

Not knowing to which one it was written, because it was as if I had written it to both, the two with the same eyes as the purpose.

15

Leaping.

The telephone call coming straight to my father's house. And from that instant that which was back in my father's eyes, that which was warm and gentle brown, that which recalled the steam of the coffee and the smell of the thick white cream and the smoke of the cigarettes, the warmth of the blazing stove. And the Royal, recalling its sound.

16

We didn't sense it at first, Grandma, but then with time we did. Over the year that followed came the letters, the greeting cards, that my father would lay on the chest by the door of the house in Reno, the letters and the greetings that spoke of them, that spoke of the five of them, that never mentioned us, any of us, any of the nineteen.

Then in the summer that followed came the gathering, the gathering of the five of them at the high-mountain camp, the gathering from which they would return smelling of dust and pine, radiant, revitalized, glowing.

By then we knew that which they knew but did not

speak of, that we bore the acrid smell, we bore the smell of the circles that had been formed on the night of your death. They had gone back to the old circle, sealing out all that were not part of its innermost core. They had gone back to the circle around the white lace in the room that was warm and glowing, the room that was not ours nor ever had been, the room to which we were now denied all entrance.

17

On a day in early spring the Xeroxed letter came from one of the nineteen, the letter that said, "We'll have our own reunion," we'll have our own. It spoke of you and Grandpa, and how we owed it to the two of you. It spoke of how we had our own relationships. It spoke of how we had our own children, how we owed it to them that they know the high-mountain land, that they know of you, and Grandpa, and one another.

It was a mob scene at the gate that led off the highway at Spooner Summit, early in the morning on the last Friday in July. There were cousins that we had not seen since the morning of your funeral, and spouses and children that we had never seen before. The four-wheelers were packed every which way into the little gravel pull-off space just outside the gate, and one of the cousins was wrestling with the lock. Then suddenly the gate swung open, and to the sound of the yipping we piled back into the vehicles and headed in.

Like instinct the silence descended inside the vehicles, as if even the smallest of the children knew it in their blood. Vehicle by vehicle the caravan rolled in, past the meadow lake that lay to the right just below the highway. We headed up into the tall, straight pines and broke onto the clearing, lush with summer, and passed the old abandoned cabin that was barely standing now, with only the sound of the engines, running in low gear, the caravan kicking up more dust than we had ever seen on the road in. We rolled through the aspen grove where the leaves were green with summer, and then upwards, along the high ridge, breaking onto the high valley floor covered with streams, specked by the wildflowers pale in color, rimmed on its far side by the mountains more massive, more bare, than we had ever seen. We passed the first patches of snow and then the first snowflower, crimson red, and then began the steepest ascent, up through the gnarled, twisted pines, past the patches of snow that were larger now, the chill of the air pouring in through the open windows. Then the ridge from which you looked down, and the sound of breaths being let out, and the yipping, ecstatic, sounding out across the valley that hid the deep blue lake.

Then the downward plunge and the swerve to the right, following the aspen that rimmed the lake, the noise of the caravan unleashed in the secrecy of the valley. And upwards, away from the lake, into the last ascent. Then the vehicles pulling off, and the motors turned off, and the doors flung open, and the good-skinned children tucked under one arm. And the flat, sandy area where we stood them beside us, and zipped their coats up to their chins, the cold, clean wind of the high mountains on their faces. And stood with them, looking out farther than you thought any human being on this earth had seen, out across the valley that hid the deep blue lake and far below it and beyond it, across the pale blue expanse that stretched out like a nursing mother to the deep blue lake, and above it, above the entirety of the earth, the Nevada sky as pure and new and blue as on the day it was first made.

In a curious way it was as if we truly thought we would find Grandpa there in the camp that lay nestled in these mountains, because as we curved around the last sandy hill and swooped down in, there was a different sound to the yipping, a frantic sound. From the open windows of the four-wheelers we looked down into the camp, and we could see the shape of the huge old stock truck in the spot from which it had not moved in forty years now, and we could see the shape of the woodpiles, dwindling but still there, surrounding the camp. We could almost smell the smoke of the campfire and the steam of the coffee filtering out through the dust and the pines.

We spent three days and two nights there, and from the instant when we had swooped down in, there had been a silent pact made, by which we would not mention them, any of the five of them. We played in the sand and in the rocks surrounding the camp, sun-warmed.

We built a fire at night and brought out red wine, and under the old stars that still shone like alabaster we told the children the simple stories of what they were. We talked of the old house, and of your silken hair, and of the kittens who looked out from the woodpile, unseen, and of the smell of rum pancakes in early morning. We talked of the days that long preceded the second funeral, that long preceded the sacrifice or the first funeral or Grandpa's stroke. We told the stories until the children were asleep in our arms, we talked long after we had tucked the children away, we talked until the night was so cold that you had to run from the fire to your bed.

18

We slept in the way that we had slept here as small children, soundly, deeply, inseparably, amidst those of the same good skin that tanned dark in summer, amidst those of the same blood.

Angelus

I

What they were. The dark-limbed child, the dark-limbed children, the links back, the untarnished links back.

Aunt Sondra in the white cotton dress. Aunt Sondra on your bed with the freshly diapered child. In the quiet of your room that held the sweet scent of your body. The child dark with summer. The child reaching, and the dance of the rosaries. Against the ring of the dining room. The angelic child. The favorite child.

Aunt Sondra on the sand, against the flow of the river. In the spot where she had lain for the three days before they found her on a Wednesday morning in early June.

What we were. What we were. What we were.

2

And by noon, the news having struck out on the telephone network, crisscrossing the country, from the little town that lay somewhere along the river named the Napa, to Washington, D.C., and back out in formation to points all over the country, ensnarling itself in the pattern of calls that had struck out from Washington, D.C., only two hours earlier. And by two the flights booked and the suitcases pulled out, and by four the planes boarded, airborne.

3

And the sequence. It was a sequence, wasn't it, Grandma, that had led here, that had wound its way to the spot by the river? Looking back you could see it, you could trace it, couldn't you, the sequence that had a beginning point and now an ending point and two years in between?

4

Their name glowing, radiant, untouched. And after twelve years of Uncle Luke's being in Washington, talk of the presidency, and the wonder of it.

And into the midst of it, hurling itself out of nowhere, the allegation. The old allegation that had lain quiet for so long that we had nearly forgotten it. That had been there in the dining room on the afternoon thirteen years past now, together with the deep blue book, and you in the window corner, silent. That had been dealt with, there in the dining room with the doors closed up. It had been dealt with, laid to rest, and now after thirteen years reappeared out of nowhere.

Recognizable, but unrecognizable, because as it had lain there unseen, beneath the buffer of thirteen years, it had grown in force, it had armed itself, it was now a palpable thing. There, undeniably there, irreversibly there on the front page of the California newspaper, the bold, black type bearing the family name and the substance of the allegation, and under it the columns of text, the cold, detached language of a newspaperman. Familiar, it had the feel of a book or an old photograph, it was something that could be held and saved and looked at a hundred years hence. But it was a distant cousin, because it had a look and a touch and a scent that was not sweet, that was strange and unsweet and lethal.

It was the beginning point, was it not, it was that which began the sequence, the two-year sequence?

4

And the shielding. The good-skinned children, the sweet-scented children, the untarnished children, the beauty of the green hills and the scent of dust and sage and gnarled pine, shielding them. They never saw it, they never touched it, they never smelled it, the black thing that could be held and saved and looked at a hundred years hence.

5

And silence. The gathering in Washington, D.C., at a place we did not know, the old circle, the circle that we could not see but which we knew was coming together. And our imagining the doors closing, our knowing that somewhere in Washington, D.C., there were doors closing, we could almost hear the sound of it. And the dreaded silence at the circle, and the sound of the first voice, halting, we could imagine the sound of it. And us waiting, there in the state which smelled of dust and sage and pine, not daring to move or breathe above the silence.

6

And then out of the silence the doors having opened up, and our imagining the voices, the crystalline ring of the voices, emerging.

And our exhaling. My father returning, and the look that was in his eyes, the look of strength and peace and promise that we knew was in all of their eyes.

And my father's words, by which we could now look back through the silence, piercing it. The words that told us of the decision to file suit in Uncle Luke's name. That told us of the decision that they were not going to sit back and let the name be bloodied after all they had worked for. That told us of how they had spoken long and hard, and how the story was an attack on all of their names, how it was an attack on the family itself. How the integrity of the family demanded that the allegation be countered head-on this time, demanded full vindication. Crystalline.

Entrusted. The name, it was entrusted to them.

And we were adults now. Nodding, and pleased to be informed. And the remembrance of the deep blue book. And the remembrance of the afternoon when it had been there, in the dining room, amidst the steam of the coffee and the smoke of the cigarettes. And you in the window corner, silent. Had it been for naught, Grandma? Was that what the denial of its existence had meant?

Leaping, they were leaping.

And the good-skinned children. Untarnished. Shielded. They knew the stories of the U-shaped house. They knew the stories of the kittens who watched from the woodpile, unseen. And the smell of rum pancakes in early morning. And the silken hair. And the music of the old language. And Grandpa bounding, disappearing. And Grandpa waving, his snow-white hair blowing. And you aproned, standing to greet the boisterous crowd that smelled of dust and pine.

7

The name regathering itself, asserting itself, cleansing itself. Returning, returning. And lodging itself, here in the midst of us, there in the clerk's office of a court building in Reno, here in the place where we lived and worked. It had its own language now, its own vocabulary, the language of *defamation* and *good name* and *good reputation*. And new defenders, the names of the eastern lawyers there beside the name that would avenge itself.

And the shielding, the good-skinned children, the good-skinned links back.

8

And we were lawyers, many of us, we knew the rules by which the case would wind its way to trial, the clear, clean rules that had to do with witnesses and depositions and motions. We knew them, we knew them, we ourselves had done a hundred of them.

9

But not this kind. Not this kind that reached so close to home, not this kind.

Reaching, the lawyers reaching, into the lining of the family, not to any of us, any of the nineteen, but to my father's generation. And backward, and inward, back to the sanctum of the dining room, invading it.

10

And the depositions bound and bearing titles, and mounting in number, until we imagined that they were stacked three feet high in the lawyers' offices. Together forming a gigantic thing, a gigantic opus, a gigantic defense that could be read a hundred years hence.

11

And the whole stream of articles now, scattered through the pages of the Reno newspapers, following it, following the case as it wound its way to trial.

And the children shielded.

12

And the name regaining itself. And the promise of victory. By all accounts, by all accounts the expectation of a multimillion-dollar verdict that would demolish the newspaper that had tarnished the name.

13

The sequence, the progression. Well, there was the piece that did not seem part of it, that did not fit within the two-year span, the little piece so incidental that it did not occur to anyone that it could be part of it, part of the two-year sequence. Aunt Sondra, the one with face and body as delicate as a porcelain doll, having taken her children and gone to Lake Tahoe, how many years ago, now? And from there, her children grown, having moved on, having resettled in San Francisco and having stayed there, and her love for the water, her need to be close to the water. And her children having said that she was happy there, she had a little boutique in Sausalito that sold women's clothes.

14

And the promise of victory. By all accounts, by all accounts. The name regaining itself.

15

Aunt Sondra at the counter in her little boutique, when the gentleman named Hans walked in, jingling the golden-colored bell that hung on the door. She knew him from her days at Tahoe, when tall, white-haired, razor-thin, almost priestlike, he had befriended her there on the front stoop of their neighboring apartments. She had been taken with his accent and his gentle manner, and over the years before she had moved on she had come to trust him, she had entrusted herself to him.

She beamed as he came through the door of the boutique, because she had not seen him in a year. She reached up to meet his embrace, and three times she said how wonderful it was to see him. She nearly danced to the coffee machine that sat on a counter in the back of the shop, delivering up two porcelain cups, steaming.

He asked her how the little boutique was faring, and he asked after her children, and over the steaming coffee she chattered on, giggling at intervals in the way that she did, still ecstatic at the sight of the familiar face. When they had downed the first cup of coffee she took the cups and headed for refills, and he excused himself momentarily, heading out the little door to fill the parking meter outside. He re-entered to the jingle of the little bell, and smiled at the fresh cup of coffee that now sat on the counter, taking it up, and sipping it.

He asked her how Uncle Francis was getting along, and he asked after Uncle Luke, and she relayed what news she had. He talked of the years when they had been neighbors, of the days when their friendship had begun. He spoke of the times when they had sat late into the evening, talking. He excused himself briefly to fill the parking meter outside.

When he reappeared he picked up where they had left off, moving gracefully from the mention of the evenings they had spent together, to her Carson City days, the stories she had told him. Well into their third cup of coffee, they laughed as she began to reminisce. He asked whether she remembered that which she had once told him, something she had thought she remembered. Oh yes, she said, and chattered on, until he interrupted her gently, excusing himself once more to fill the parking meter outside.

He returned once again, as the steam of the fresh pot of coffee was filling up the little boutique, and as she served up the fresh cups she had forgotten what they had left off talking about. He brought the conversation back gently, asking her more questions about what she thought had taken place, what she thought she remembered. He listened quietly, gently, as she picked up where she had left off.

He had filled the parking meter twice more by the time the next hour had waned. He said gently that it was time for him to be on his way, and meeting his embrace she said how wonderful the afternoon had been, what a breath of fresh air to see him come through the door.

She closed the boutique early that day, and strolled the little sidewalks with the warmth of the afternoon running through her. She didn't smell a thing.

16

The motion to retake deposition was filed two days later by the lawyers for the California newspaper, lodging itself there with the name in the court building in Reno, together with a sealed envelope containing the tapes, the original of their typed transcription, and the signed affidavit of the white-haired gentleman. By the next morning the news having hit the newspapers, and our reading it, there at the breakfast table in early morning, our reading the article in which Aunt Sondra's name was printed and reprinted twenty times over, our reading the words that spoke of the initial deposition Aunt Sondra had given, and the words that spoke of the taped conversation, and the words that spoke of an alleged conflict between the two, the black words, the new black words. Even in the safey of our own homes we could feel the storm that was rolling in, twisting, swirling. Recalling the U-shaped house, and the sound of the front door swinging shut, and the sound of the inner door swinging shut, and the huddling, there at the table covered with white lace.

17

And the children shielded.

18

It was as familiar to us as instinct by now, the silence that settled in around us, the silence under which we could not see, over which, for four days, we barely moved or breathed.

We knew that Aunt Sondra's second deposition had been taken on Friday, that she had appeared at a law office in San Francisco and it had gone forward. We knew that after it she had taken her car and gone, but where or how far none of us knew, not even her children knew. From Saturday to Wednesday the silence hung around us, thick.

When the telephone message struck out from Washington, D.C., on Wednesday, connecting the east coast midmorning with the western dawn, we thought we had sprung free from the silence, glowing. *It's over*, the message said, *the suit settled this morning*. In our minds we could feel the warmth of celebration. We exhaled deep breaths, and moved, nearly danced, through the early morning hours.

There was something in us like a superstition that later said if only we hadn't exhaled, if only we had held on just a day more, the second message, the one that struck out from the little town somewhere along the Napa, would not have come. But it did come, timed like clockwork, it lit out into the morning with all of the unexpectedness of an ingenious prank, the hint of a smile to its voice, ensnarling itself in the pattern of calls that had struck out from Washington, D.C., only two hours earlier. There were family who had not even heard the message from Washington yet, who had return-call messages waiting and picked up the telephone and dialed, and heard all in one tangled, twisted sentence that the libel suit settled, it's over, full vindication of the name, and Aunt Sondra, Aunt Sondra, found on a beach somewhere along the Napa, some fishermen found her, she had been there since Sunday morning, she had taken her own life.

19

Then the strange, quick, miraculous untangling, the newspaper stories that appeared the next morning, the article that spoke of the suit and the settlement and the vindication of the name, and on an altogether separate page the article originating from the little town somewhere along the Napa, bearing no reference to the first article, unrelated.

And the name glowing, radiant.

And the children shielded.

20

There had been a second taping.

It was the first beach day on the shore of Lake Tahoe when the small group of cousins sat on the sand and looked out onto the enormous pale blue expanse of the lake and the endless clear blue of the Nevada sky and played the tape by which we could now see back through the silence, we could see right through back to Sunday morning six days past, we could see right through to the little motel room on Sunday morning on the edge of the town somewhere along the Napa River.

We sat cross-legged like children and felt the early, high sun on our limbs as it washed us, cleansed us, of the place we had passed through yet once more. We breathed in the high air and the sun and the endless blueness, cleansing ourselves of the church into which we had walked with our heads held high, where there had been only a trickling of people this time, those few with the old familiar faces who could not *not* have been there. The crowd had smelled it this time, they had smelled it for five hundred miles in all directions.

There on the shore of the lake we listened to the click of the cassette recorder and then the *click* by which we were let into the little motel room on Sunday morning somewhere along the Napa River, and mixed in with the sound of the afternoon waves lapping against the shore we heard the opening of a cupboard and then the flick of a cigarette lighter. Then the voice that spoke to her children, that followed the rhythm of childbirth, that like the rhythm of childbirth began haltingly, apprehensively.

Then silence.

Click. Click.

And then the evening. The voice that took command, that calmed the child, that prepared it, coaxed it, that spoke of the miracle of birth, that spoke of the miracle of life, that spoke of separateness, that spoke of responsibility to self, that spoke of the health of the human soul.

Then silence.

Click. Click.

Then the cold, low voice. That spoke of how the lawsuit was not hers and how the name was not hers. How she had no duty to them or to the name. How she had breached no duty. How she had betrayed no duty.

Click.

Click.

Then the sweetening, the wet, warm, flooding voice of the mother at the instant of separation, the voice as pure and radiant as the air that came off of the spring-swollen lake. That spoke of the water, that spoke of her love for the water. That spoke of the enormous blue lake called Tahoe. That spoke to her children of the spot she had chosen, that would have no meaning for them, that they would never have to see or think of again. That spoke of leaving the enormous pale blue lake pure, unsullied, free of all but sun and water. That spoke of how the water had nurtured her, how it would nurture them.

Click.

We sat cross-legged, squinting at the afternoon sun as we looked out across the lake. The golden word was there, it was dancing on the waves.

21

We made the trek to the high-mountain camp, the second reunion of cousins, barely a month after the death by the river, and it had been a matter of just being there, around the five that were the youngest of us, those still dazed, stunned, half numb.

We met at the gate and headed in, following the road along the meadow lake, past the old cabin and the straight pines and the aspen, along the high ridge and the high meadow and up through the gnarled pines. We reached the high crest from which you exhaled as you looked down at the hidden lake, deep blue, and there was no yipping this time, only the sound of the motors cutting out across the valley. We headed down and took the right curve upward, passing the high lookout point without stopping.

We came around the last sandy curve, and headed down into the camp and parked the four-wheelers in silence, and it was by instinct that we knew that the pact that had enabled the reunion past had grown, had swelled. We stepped out of the vehicles into a camp that was like a minefield of forbidden subjects.

We cooked and ate and chopped wood in the quiet of the camp, and at night we gathered at the fire and watched it burn. We huddled at the fire as the five of them came and went aimlessly, approaching and then withdrawing from the fire and the group around it. Later we lay in the dark listening to the sound of their footsteps, wandering through the camp, wandering through the remains of the woodpiles, as if they were searching for something.

We went away believing in our minds that maybe the death by the river had been a sacred thing, maybe it had been that which like a clear message would speak to the creature called family, would speak to it of things as simple as water and sky, of things as simple as the smell of the dust and the pines. In our minds we knew the message was there, the unmistakable message by which all that was good and true, as real as birth and life and good skin and death, cried out, screamed out, from beneath the name. We went away thinking that in the quiet of the camp there was a mending that had begun.

22

But the name, Grandma, it had regained itself, and it was out there, it had lit back out from here and it was indomitable now.

And talk of the presidency, and the wonder of it. And the *immigrant father* and the *immigrant mother* and the *green hills* and the *sheep camps* and the *boarding house* and the *brood of five*. The immigrant story. Vindicated. Unrestrained. Glowing. And the crowd reforming itself.

23

And then the third gathering of cousins, the convergence at the gate on a morning in late July, and the heading in.

There was an excitement among us, as though the two years that had elapsed since the last of the reunions had created a buffer between us and the river. There were things to talk about now, safe things like what have you been doing since the last reunion, and how the children have grown in two years. We made the slow trek inwards, and at the crest from which we looked down on the deep blue lake the yipping cut loose. We headed downwards, and upwards, and at the high lookout point we pulled off and got out of the vehicles and looked out.

We cooked a huge dinner that night, and later we brought out the red wine and gathered up our children and settled into the circle around the fire, and talked and told jokes and sang. One by one the children fell into sleep by the glow of the fire, and one by one we lifted them and carried them off and tucked them away and came back to the circle.

The jokes and the songs subsided, and the talk took over, and there by the fire under the old stars we told the old stories of the old house, and the pancakes, and the kittens, and your silken hair. Then slowly, unnoticeably, the conversation moved out of the early years, we were talking of the red beret years, we were laughing, recalling the broad-smile faces that had flooded the dining room. Then suddenly we were moving forward further still, we were talking about the first funeral, and then suddenly we were talking about the second campaign, and then suddenly we were talking about the name. Then the crack, the sentence that tore through the circle around the campfire, coming out of nowhere but in retrospect so logical. How the name glowed. Someone said how their name glowed.

Reaching, the dark limbs reaching, and touching the rosaries, and rattling them, and the quiet of your room, and the warm scent of you, the dark limbs beside the white cotton dress against the crystalline ring. The angelic one, the favorite one, the angelic one.

Rising, and in the glow of the firelight we could see his face clearly, the face twenty-eight years old now, the age of the faces that had encircled the dining room table in the years when we had played in the underneath. He stood there, helpless, unable to speak, and then into the angelic face flooded that which the buffer of time had wrought, the blood-spattered rage that had come out of the death by the river, that had come out of the loss of the valuable thing, filling the round eyes, turning them from brown to black, blacker than any eyes we had ever seen. Then finally the sound of his voice, ripping through the firelight and out through the dark night of the mountains and upwards, toward the old stars, like the first enraged scream of the infant held up, the cord cut, blood-spattered.

Then the silence that flowed out of the breach of the pact of silence, the empty, barren, fractured silence in the camp that night and the next day and the next night.

24

And the acrid smell. The camp covered with it. And the children, the good-skinned children, covered with it.

The Golden Mind

I

The swirling, there in the darkness, the chaos in the underneath, hidden, us there in it, in the midst of it, we are it. Unseen. They cannot see us. They cannot see us.

And glowing, the thing that we now recognized, the thing that we now knew was it, the thing that had lingered there, carved there in the old stone, ancient, ancient, that had followed us here and planted itself here, at the center, hovering, above the white lace, atop the sacred table, entrusting us, entrusting us to itself, glowing.

Wrecking them, devouring them, the things that

shone in the light of day, the safe calm of the dining room and the book and the lovely rhythm and the color of the aspen and even the place that smelled of dust and pine and even the one in the white cotton dress the one that could be any of ours and even the angelic face and even the good skin, the warm dark skin wrecked, and the very thing for which the glowing thing stood, the sweet good thing called family, wrecked, the trove of valuable things that ran there in the limbs of the underneath, the trove of things that were theirs not ours and yet they were us they were us they *were* us, what have we what have we what have we for our own children and theirs?

2

Is that not it, Grandma, is that not it?

Are we the ones to whom the entrustment ran? Are we the ones, are we the ones to whom you entrusted them? The five of them and the things that shone, the circle and the book and the rhythm and the sunlit color and the smell of the dust and pine and the promise and the good-skinned children, the good-skinned links back, Grandma? Are we the fiduciaries, Grandma? Did we fail in the rescue, Grandma? Have we done even worse than that, Grandma, have we sullied and tarnished? Are we the ones against which the circle formed, are we the dreaded ones? Are we the ones who would make bad of good?

Is our breach in not seeing what they see, Grandma? Or in seeing what they do not?

3

But my father, Grandma, your own second-born, he had seen it, he had seen it, he had seen it. He had seen it in early morning, there in early morning as the mist of the green hills rose up and spread and cleared to the crystal notes of the *txistu*, he had seen it as clear as day, had he not, Grandma? Because he had seen the splendor of the *Zamalzain*, there in early morning against the greenness of the hills, he had seen the white lace that spread out around him and the half-full glass below it, and he had seen the miracle feet, the miracle feat. And in seeing that he saw this too, did he not, Grandma, he could not have seen the unspilled half-full glass without seeing in it the potential for its spilling, he could not have not seen it, implicit, that which is now beneath the white lace, he could not have not seen the little glass lying on its side, the dark red color spread out around it.

And he had wrapped it in yellow gold, the color of sunlight, the color of aspen in fall, and he had handed it to us, he had entrusted it to us. Long ago, Grandma, long ago he had seen it, hadn't he, he had seen what we see only now?

4

And your youngest, Grandma, Uncle Francis, your baby of the five, the light of the new world. He had seen it, he had seen it as clear as day, had he not, Grandma?

5

The dissertation, the *brilliant dissertation*, it was on a day in winter that I found it, Grandma, barely visible there in the row of books that lined my father's shelves, faded white on its edge, unlabeled. Browsing there on a Saturday afternoon I happened to pull it, and glance down at its cover, and see the title, and Uncle Francis's name, and the date over thirty years old, there in the rough, obsolete type of the old manual machines. Romeo and Juliet, he had written of them.

I took it, and a month later sat down one evening and turned to its first page and began reading, and by the end of the first paragraph I knew one thing, I knew that he had the gift of language, not the gift of poetry that my father had, but the gift of language that was clean, concise, rational, unemotional, like the language of the law. And then by the end of the first chapter I knew also that the greater thing was true, he had the mind of enlightenment, Grandma, he had the clean, pure mind that saw things that others could not, that saw reason and order where others could not.

In careful sequence he outlined the traditional body of thought that surrounded Shakespeare's love story. It was not tragedy, the scholars had written, because the protagonists who in the end took their own lives in the dim light of the tomb were half-children, innocents, lacking in any tragic flaw. The play was artistic failure, the scholars said, it was a tale of adolescents whose fates were attributable to nothing more meaningful than an unfortunate series of missed communications, nothing more meaningful than accident. *It is the purpose of this dissertation,* the initial chapter concluded, *to show otherwise.*

I placed a marker at the end of the first chapter, and the next night I opened it up again, and read to the end of the second chapter. He spoke now of the scholars who had searched for tragic element in the story of the lovers, of the scholars who, here or there, thought they had found it. One by one he quoted them, the scholar who pointed to the "sensual bias" of Juliet's love, to the "unbalanced, unrestrained spirit" of Romeo, the scholar who pointed to the stubbornness, the defiant arrogance, of each. One by one he refuted them, pointed to the positive light, the pure and untarnished light, in which Shakespeare had painted the adolescents' love. I moved the marker to the end of the second chapter and put the dissertation back on the shelf.

On the third night I sat down again, and took the marker out, and moved on into the third chapter, and suddenly I was not just reading, I was staring down at the page, there in a room that suddenly felt cold, freezing cold. I heard the crystalline voice that had encircled the underneath in the days that now seemed too long past to have been real. I heard the voice of the golden, lucid mind that as we played in the underneath had come and gone from the typewriter, writing of Shakespeare's love story, writing of the tragic element that was there in the story's true characters, that was there in the characters of the families, the strong families, the element by which fortune had taken its unseen turn, the element that led to the catastrophe, that led to the accident that was no accident, that led to the loss of the characters' own most valuable things. He was speaking to us, Grandma, the voice that was the youngest of them, young and gleaming. He was speaking to us right through the thick, grey layer that spread over thirty years, piercing it.

6

He had seen it, Grandma, he had seen it there in the safe calm of the dining room filled with the steam of the fresh coffee and the smell of the thick white cream and the smoke of the cigarettes, he had seen beneath the white lace and like a visionary he had seen what was coming, what was coming. And if he had seen it then, Grandma, how could he not see it now?

7

The half-full glass, the half-full glass, what I did not know was the same thing I had not known at twelve years old, the same thing that on the morning at the *fronton* had run through my mind all mixed in with the notes of the *txistu*, whether the spilling of the wine *was* the disaster, or whether, like a crystal ball, it was that which *told* of disaster, disaster lurking, hidden beneath the green hills. I had never known the true nature of the *Zamalzain*, whether his feet controlled the fate of the valley, whether they carried power and drew blame, or whether he was pure visionary, with no real power except that his feet could see what others could not, could speak as others could not.

I thought of the creature called family, and the wine glass, and the dark red color, and I asked the same question, Grandma, the same. I looked back on the death by the river, and I knew, Grandma, I knew that like the lovers' death it had been both, it had been disaster, but disaster which told of disaster, no accident, no accident. I looked back further, Grandma, I looked back on that which had preceded it, and I knew that it was more than a two-year sequence, more than that. I looked back to the rift, Grandma, the unimaginable rift between blood and the mending and the reforming of the circle and the huddle so threatened, so defensive as to insist on the unimaginable exclusion of blood itself, and I knew, I knew, that the sequence, the two-year sequence had flowed from there, it had sprung from there. And further, further back, I looked back to that which had preceded the rift, I looked back, back, back to the afternoon when the deep blue book was given up, back to the afternoon when we were locked there in the dining room and you in the window corner, silent, and you had seen it, you had seen beneath the white lace and you had seen the glass on its side and the dark red color spread out around it, irretrievable, irretrievable.

And I knew, I knew, I knew that from that moment we had been leaping, Grandma, leaping above that which we could not see beneath the white lace, all of us, all of us.

8

Go back, go back, go back. You in the window corner, silent. And the image of the deep blue book. And the voices crystalline. But before that, Grandma, even before that. The thread of distance. The thread of distance. And Grandpa in the quiet of the far back bedroom. Could it have been done *then*, Grandma, could we even then have been leaping above a disaster we could not see?

I thought back further, Grandma, I looked back beyond the afternoon when the deep blue book had been given up. I looked back on the black allegation in defense against which the sacrifice had been made, and on the second campaign, gleaming, into which the allegation had been shot. I thought back further, I thought back on the year when Grandpa had lain dying, and on the five who had never known grandparents, who had never before seen death and could not see the beauty that was there in it before their own eyes, and I knew that the campaign, gleaming, had flowed out of that year, it had sprung from that year. I thought back even further, I thought back to the first campaign summer when the ceremonial red berets were passed out by the hundreds, when the crowd of faces had been allowed entry into the sanctum of the dining room, and I knew that the second campaign, and all that came with it and after it, had sprung from there too. I thought back to the immigrant story that was new and clean, and how the first campaign had grown out of it, had sprung from it. I thought of the deep blue book, untarnished, untouched, and how the immigrant story had sprung from it. I thought back on the gathering when the typed pages were read, and on the approval and the celebration which flowed from approval, and I knew that from there all else had sprung. I thought of the gathering of the children of immigrants, the huddle at the dining room table, safe, and I knew that all that came later had sprung from there. I thought of the brown-and-white print, the portrait without grandparents, the little family alone, alone, alone in a new land, and somehow I knew that it had all flowed from there, it had sprung from there.

Then I thought back even further, back to that which ran in the blood of the children in the brown-and-white print, back to that which lay beneath the veil of space and time through which they could not see. I thought back on the green hills, I thought back on the acrid smell, on the tunnels woven like the limbs of a jungle through the dark earth, on the raging beast that lived in the depth of the underneath. I thought back on the ten thousand years of not daring to move or breathe over the dark earth.

9

I thought of the rosaries, the old dark rosaries that hung from your bedpost, and the group of us there in the quiet of your room, hovering, and the child reaching, and the sound of the rosaries, the dance of the rosaries in the quiet of your room. It was a clicking sound, was it not, Grandma? Even then it was a clicking sound.

10

And you in the corner by the window in the quiet of the afternoon, sipping, sipping the milkshake, and the timeless intervals.

11

And the warm scent of you, the good scent of you, the touch of your hair in evening, that was silken, that flowed in silver waves down the front of you, more beautiful than anything we know, even now, even now.

The Visit to the Sheep Ranch

I

For years we had talked of it, the day trip that we should make out to the ranches that spotted the hills to the southeast, in March, at lambing season. My children had been raised in Reno, a town which over the years had outgrown its epithet, so that it was now the littlest big city in the world, if not even larger than that. Each year my father had said how we had to get the children out to the lambing corrals this time, how the ranches that still ran sheep were dwindling, how they would be gone in a matter of a few years without the children having known their heritage. Each year we had agreed, and then before we knew it March had come and gone.

That we finally did make the trip may have had something to do with Admission Day, which had come five months earlier, in late October. It had been years since we had attended the annual parade in Carson City, but this year my father had been selected grand marshal, and he and my mother were set to ride at the front in a restored Model T. My sister and I figured that our children should ride with them, we figured they were entitled to a taste of notoriety, and they sure would never get it from us.

So we dressed them in Levi's and drove them to Carson early on the morning of Admission Day, meeting up with my parents at the designated spot and piling the children into the bumper seat of the restored Model T. We parked the car five blocks off of Main, and made our way on foot to the steps of one of the old court buildings just south of the capitol grounds. From amidst the crowd we waved and snapped photographs as they passed by.

We left the parade before it was half over, in order to find the car and make it to the finish spot before the crowd dispersed. We headed down the steps of the old court building and veered left, away from Main, into the back streets of old Carson City. We headed north, in the general direction of the spot where we had left the car, and somehow we ended up on the old street. We walked quietly, on the sidewalks beneath the old trees golden with autumn, and we could still hear the hum of the crowd that lined Main.

We slowed our pace as we approached the old house, and when we were on the sidewalk dead in front of it we stopped, and stood looking at it. Finally one of us said how shabby it looked, how the paint was peeling off all over, how you would roll over in your grave if you could see it now. We were standing there when suddenly we noticed the presence of a man, fifty or so in age, just inside the gate, on the other side of the hedge, and in a friendly tone he asked if he could help us.

We turned red-faced, and apologized for the intrusion into his morning, and proceeded to explain that we knew the house, our grandparents used to live here. When he heard this he beamed, and said how he admired the family, and then suddenly he turned red-faced, and apologized for the exterior which he had been meaning to get to, and explained that they had been refurbishing the interior, and wouldn't we like to see the inside? We jumped at the chance, and strode through the little gate as he opened it.

We followed him up the two steps, through the old screen door and across the front porch, and as he turned the old brass knob and opened the old wooden door there appeared the figure of a woman, roughly the same age as the man. He introduced her as his wife, and with a renewed beam on his face explained to the woman who we were, and she welcomed us in.

It was a physical thing as we crossed the threshold into the darkness of the entryway, the musty smell which through time we had forgotten, that was still here in the entryway, living here, engrained in its walls. The couple must have seen us sniffing it like dogs on the trail of a scent. Then in the dim light of the entryway my sister turned to me and said, "Do you smell it?" and the poor woman nearly jumped with embarrassment, launching into a frantic explanation of how the cats came here, how she tried to keep them out but how they seemed to like it here, how she knew there must be a problem with the smell but with the cats always around she really couldn't rely on herself to detect it. We assured her that no, there was no bad smell here, we were speaking of a different smell, a smell that we recognized from childhood. She stared at us, uncomprehending, as though unable to reconcile the image of people sniffing after smells with the image of the successful family whose house she had bought.

They steered us to the right, into the front room of the apartment, and it was there in the sunlit room that was unchanged, that the old feeling started up again, the sickening feeling, grey in color. We moved into the middle room of the apartment, following the U of the house in reverse direction, and I turned toward my sister and saw that she too had become silent, wide-eyed. There in the second unchanged room, against the backdrop of the couple who had ensnared us, a sense of panic began to thread itself into the greyness. As we reached the kitchen of the apartment the panic turned into terror, raw, cold terror at the thought of the room we were drawing near to, terror at the thought of the table, terror at the thought of the chair in the corner by the window, terror at the thought of the soul that would be there in the corner by the window, that had been there, we now knew, for all these years, waiting for us to come back. By the time we emerged into the little patio that caught the late-morning sun, the terror had turned into a swirling thing.

The woman was speaking a hundred miles an hour as she opened the screen door into the kitchen, and we followed her like automatons, not speaking or even thinking. The hum of her voice kept on as we crossed through the kitchen that was unchanged, and as she reached the open doorway that led into the dining room the hum grew more distant, then inaudible. We took the steps that led to the doorway, and reached the doorway, and looked straight into the dining room, straight in onto the miracle of it.

There was no table. There in the spot where we had played in the underneath there was carpet, bare carpet, new, strewn with the gift boxes and wrapping paper and ribbons of a woman who had an early start on Christmas. There was no chair by the window, there was nothing but carpet fit to the corner and the sunlight streaming in. The walls were papered in flowers, and more rolls of the same wallpaper were leaned against the inside wall. There was no smell of fresh coffee, no smell of thick white cream, there was no cigarette smoke. There was no greyness, no panic, no terror, no swirling.

2

We left Reno early in the morning on the third Sunday in March, the children packed into the back of my father's old four-wheeler, and headed south twenty miles past Carson, then southeast across the desert hills, through the little town of Wellington. We had lucked out on the weather, my father said. He could remember the grueling ordeal of lambing in snow. It was a clear day, the first warmth of spring in the air, the Nevada sky as blue as we had ever remembered it.

The rancher was expecting us, and he was standing outside in the morning sun as we came driving up the dirt road that led to the ranch house. He was of old English stock, my father had told us, the ranch had been in his family for three generations. From a distance we could see his tall, lanky build, his thick white hair beneath the old western hat. My father said he was the last of a vanishing breed.

From where we piled out of the car in front of the ranch house we could see the enormous spread of corrals and see the thousands of sheep that filled them, and we could see the dark figures of the herders, Peruvian, perched here and there on the rails. We fastened our jackets and followed the rancher in the direction of the corrals. We were wise to have come today, he said, there was only one last group to go.

He led us, and with the opening of the first gate came the smell of the old wood, mixed with the dust, mixed with the old smell of the sheep, mixed with the spring sun. We headed in, through a maze of a hundred tiny pens, each of the pens holding a ewe and her newborn, nursing quietly for the few brief hours, the rancher said, before being turned out with the herd. We slowed our pace and moved to one side of the walkway as we approached that which we had not anticipated, the twisted little body of a dead lamb, and then another, and another, pulled from the pen and then left there on the ground, dust-covered from the foot traffic that had passed through. The rancher must have noticed the change in our pace, because he turned silent, leading the way onward, until finally he spoke and said how they always lost a few, there was nothing they could do.

We emerged from the pens onto a string of corrals that must have held five hundred ewes each, together with their young. We followed the rancher past corral after corral, my father reaching out to shake the hands of the dark herders perched here and there along the rails. We reached the last in the string of corrals, which held the last holdouts, a hundred or so big-bellied ewes milling in the dust, nervous, stamping at our approach. They were mostly first-time mothers, the rancher said. They had the hardest time of it.

With the rancher we climbed onto the old wooden rails and sat perched above the ewes. We focused in on one of them, who had headed off alone to a far corner of the corral, who stood frantically pawing the ground, then kneeling, rolling onto her side, then scrambling back up to her feet. She would be next, the rancher said, it was a matter of twenty minutes at the outside.

But then not one minute later the rancher said he took it back, there was one coming right now, and we turned our eyes in the direction in which his outstretched arm was pointing. There on the opposite side of the corral, not fifteen feet from us, a group of ewes had backed away from one that now stood alone, planted there, her rear haunches slightly outstretched, unable to move.

We watched, until suddenly between her haunches you could see a fluff of white, snow-white, pure white, white that made the ewe's coat look dingy, not white at all. Then the fluff of white took shape, the perfect little shape of the lamb's head, wide-eyed, looking out. Then the first act by which the lamb delivered itself, pulling his own front legs out from under him, stretching them forward, into the air. Then the mother ewe, she took three steps forward, the lamb hanging there, half-delivered, between her haunches. Three more steps, and the lamb just fell out of her, landing square on his face in the dust. Then onward, the wondrous blue-red cord trailing from her haunches, then the miracle of the placenta, the color of clear water streaked with red, streaked with blue, hanging from her as she stepped forward, until finally it too fell to the ground, and she was free of it.

Then the turn-about, the ewe fifteen feet from the lamb, facing it, looking at it, the lamb on its front knees, struggling to rise, falling onto its face, struggling again. Then the ewe's first step toward the lamb, unsure, hesitating, and the slow walk, reaching the lamb, standing there beside it, not even looking at it. Then the ewe looking down at the lamb, and the first irrevocable act, the sniffing, the ewe's nose scanning the snow-white fluff, searching out the smell by which she would know her own in a herd of a thousand.

We watched the ewe and her newborn, until suddenly we noticed that the rancher was looking elsewhere, he was looking back to the far corner of the corral. The ewe that we had thought would be the first this morning was on her side now, lying outstretched in the dust, struggling. We heard the sharp sound of the rancher's voice, we saw the dark herders leap down from the rails and come running. We saw the rancher and the herders converge on the ewe, we saw a herder take hold of her hind legs, we saw the rancher roll up his sleeve, reach in between her haunches, far in, to his elbow. We saw the rancher look up to the faces of the herders, and from a distance we could see him speaking to them. We saw the outstretched body of the ewe lying motionless in the dust, we saw the gleam of the knife as it was pulled from a sheath, and then we turned our gaze back, back to the ewe who stood beside the white lamb.

3

The rancher was carrying it in his arms as he approached us, his worn western boots kicking up dust as he crossed the open space of the corral. There was a weary look to his face, mixed with a sweetness, a tenderness. He held the lamb close against his chest, his arms cradling it, its legs stretching downward. The wool of the lamb was soaked in blood, and the rancher too, his hands and his forearms and his workshirt were drenched with it, still bright red, still wet. When he reached the spot where we sat perched on the rails, he stood holding the lamb, and then he looked up to us, squinting at the late-morning sun. "It's what we call a bummer," he said. "If he survives the first two weeks, he'll live through anything. Those that do are the toughest, their line'll be the toughest. Toughest little rascals in the herd."

I was looking down at the rancher and the cradled lamb, the smell of the dust all blended in with the smell of the old rails and the sound of the ewes bleating, and the blue, the incredible blue of the Nevada sky, and there began the unraveling, the dust and the smell of the old wood and the bleating, the clear blue and the face of the rancher and the cradling of the lamb splitting up into fragments, disconnecting. I scanned the expanse of the corral, then again, and again, but still I could not get the scene back into focus, the fragments reconnected.

Then I looked to the side of me, I looked down the stretch of the old rails, and there framed against the blue of the desert sky were two faces, in profile, looking downward to the rancher as he spoke, and in them the morning, and all that encircled the morning, reconnected itself.

I looked at the face of my father, that even still carried in it the warmth of the dark earth, the face in which the old earth and the beauty of the green hills, the unspoiled heritage and the circle and the promise and the name, the dust and the white unspattered lamb and the old wood and the clear sky, and the untarnished beauty of this morning and of all mornings that had preceded it and would come after it, were still blended together, tied together, pulling at each other, needing each other.

Then I looked at the other face, the face framed against my father's face, the face of a twelve-year-old, the good-skinned twelve-year-old. The purpose. The link back. I looked at the young face and suddenly I knew that I had never looked at it before, the face that bore nothing of the green hills, nothing of the dark earth, the face that was as open, as unrestrained, as free as these desert hills.

I looked at the young face and suddenly, for the first time in the twelve years of its coming of age, it dawned on me that it had never even known the dark haven of the underneath. It had never even known the smell of the pancakes or the magical sound of the old language, or the taste of champagne in midafternoon, the imagined rescue of a book in the midst of fire. I looked at the face and for the first time I knew, I knew, that it did not need the view down on the deep blue jewel and the pale blue expanse beyond it to see clearly. It did not need the closeness of the good skin to sleep soundly.

I looked at the face of the boy and then at the face of his younger sister, I looked at the two young faces that of all of us had not turned their gaze from the far corner of the corral. They had watched it, they had breathed and moved right through it.

I thought of the empty space where the table had been, and of the new carpet stretched across it, and of sunlight the color of aspen in fall, flooding the room.

I thought of the view from the graves that looked to these desert hills, to the morning when we would return here.

I thought of the ten thousand years.

I thought of the beast that lay slain.

4

You knew. You did not know these young faces and yet you knew that someday they would be here, you knew what they would look like.

You knew the wine glass was there. You knew it long ago, you knew it raven-haired, gold-earringed, you knew it before leaving the green hills. You willed it. You kicked it over. It was no accident.

And that *was* it, wasn't it, Grandma? The sequence. The rescue. The entrustment. We were entrusted to you.

5

And the warm scent of your good body, it is untouched.

THE BASQUE SERIES

A Book of the Basques, *Rodney Gallop*
In a Hundred Graves: A Basque Portrait, *Robert Laxalt*
Basque Nationalism, *Stanley G. Payne*
Amerikanuak: Basques in the New World, *William A. Douglass and Jon Bilbao*
Beltran: Basque Sheepman of the American West, *Beltran Paris, as told to William A. Douglass*
The Basques: The Franco Years and Beyond, *Robert P. Clark*
The Witches' Advocate: Basque Witchcraft and the Spanish Inquisition (1609–1614), *Gustav Henningsen*
Navarra: The Durable Kingdom, *Rachel Bard*
The Guernica Generation: Basque Refugee Children of the Spanish Civil War, *Dorothy Legarreta*

Basque Sheepherders of the American West, *photographs by Richard H. Lane, text by William A. Douglass*

A Cup of Tea in Pamplona, *Robert Laxalt*

Sweet Promised Land, *Robert Laxalt*

Traditional Basque Cooking: History and Preparation, *José María Busca Isusi*

Basque Violence: Metaphor and Sacrament, *Joseba Zulaika*

Basque-English Dictionary, *Gorka Aulestia*

The Basque Hotel, *Robert Laxalt*

Vizcaya on the Eve of Carlism: Politics and Society, 1800–1833, *Renato Barahona*

Contemporary Basque Fiction: An Anthology, *Jesús María Lasagabaster*

A Time We Knew: Images of Yesterday in the Basque Homeland, *photographs by William Albert Allard, text by Robert Laxalt*

English-Basque Dictionary, *Gorka Aulestia and Linda White*

Negotiating with ETA: Obstacles to Peace in the Basque Country, 1975–1988, *Robert P. Clark*

Escape via Berlin: Eluding Franco in Hitler's Europe, *José Antonio de Aguirre; introduction by Robert P. Clark*

A Rebellious People: Basques, Protests, and Politics, *Cyrus Ernesto Zirakzadeh*

A View from the Witch's Cave: Folktales of the Pyrenees, *edited by Luis de Barandiarán Irizar*

Child of the Holy Ghost, *Robert Laxalt*

The Deep Blue Memory, *Monique Urza*